The Man without Shelter

Indrajit GARAI

Legal Notices

Copyright © 2022 by Indrajit GARAI. All rights are reserved by the author.

Copyright deposited with the Legal Deposit at the National Library of France, and with the Copyright Office at the Library of Congress in the United States of America.

The violation of copyright is a federal offense punished by the law. No parts of this book can be copied, reproduced, transmitted without prior permission from the author.

Published by Indrajit GARAI, September 2022

This is a work of fiction. All characters and events portrayed in this work are results of author's imagination alone. The names of certain places and institutions may be real, but any eventual resemblances to actual persons (living or dead), incidents, times, and places are entirely accidental and involuntary.

For Estelle and Mylène

1

The key turned twice in the lock. Arnault set the book aside and sat up on his bunk. The guard didn't stand at the door this time; she entered his cell, stood across his bunk, and smiled at him with more than her usual warmth. No other guard stood on the corridor outside.

"Pack your stuff," she said.

"Why?"

"The warden asked."

"Everything?"

"Yes."

"A transfer?"

"He'll tell you."

Arnault gathered his belongings and squeezed them into his duffle bag. The guard asked him to leave the books on the table; she would return those to the library. He slung the bag over his shoulder then held out his wrists to her.

She shook her head, sighed, and pushed his wrists down.

The long balcony looked over the hall sleeping below. The silence from all sides announced the hour. Their footsteps on the corridor woke the guard on the bench outside the interview rooms; he lifted his head, recognized Arnault, and waved. They went past the security door, took the stairs down, and headed toward the warden's office.

The bell from the chapel chimed eleven times.

The warden's cheeks bore pillow marks, but his face didn't appear sleepy. His hair was disheveled, and his eyes were alert. He looked up from the file opened before him, reached for the knot of his tie, and realized it wasn't there. He rubbed his neck, greeted Arnault, and pointed to the seat across his desk.

"We're releasing you," the warden said.

"When?"

"Now."

"At this hour?"

"At this minute."

"Why?"

"By order from the authorities."

The warden informed the fax he had just received called for Arnault's release before the term. For reason, it only stated the evidences no longer sufficed to hold him in detention; if Arnault wanted to know more, he would have to contact his lawyer tomorrow morning. The warden signed the authorization for Arnault's release, had him sign it too, and then handed it over to the guard.

"Do I have to leave right now?" Arnault asked.

"The order is for immediate release," the warden said. "And unconditional. We don't have rights to hold you a minute longer. Do you have a place to go to?"

"No."

"What about your parents?"

"The last time I heard from them was twenty years ago."

"Any relatives who could take you in?"

"Not that I know of."

The warden regretted, if it were up to him, he would let Arnault stay in his cell until tomorrow morning, but the fax that had pulled him out of his bed didn't leave him a choice. Unlike other penitentiaries, this high security prison had no guest rooms either. There were no hotels around, but, down the road, there was a shelter for the homeless; if Arnault wanted to spend the night there, the warden could call them now and secure him a place.

Arnault thanked him for the offer and said he would check this place out himself.

The warden added that Arnault's clothes from twenty-three years ago wouldn't fit him anymore. He had sent a set of his own clothes to the cloakroom; if Arnault wanted, he could take the set from there, along with his wages for these years and the rest of his stuff from before. He agreed the way Arnault was being released onto the streets at this hour was absurd, but he could do nothing about it. He assured he would have plenty of good things to say about Arnault's character, if he ever needed references for a job or anything else.

Arnault thanked him for his kindness.

The warden warned that most convicts made their first mistake right out of prison, but he also knew that Arnault didn't belong to this kind. He believed, with the help of a social worker if necessary, Arnault would soon find his way back into the civil society again. With the skills he had learnt in the prison's workshop, he would find a job soon and make the best of his remaining life; he was only forty-two, and he had a long way ahead of him to go. The warden rose from his seat, shook Arnault's hand, wished him good luck in reentering life, and asked the guard to accompany him till the exit door.

The cloakroom clerk handed Arnault his old clothes and belt, his schoolbag, his state ID with the photo of him nineteen years old, his wallet, and his monies in franc that no longer circulated in France. Arnault gathered all his belongings, from now and from before, took the clothes and the jacket from the warden, and then went into a cabin to change.

He was about to shove his old clothes into the schoolbag, when he noticed the blood stains on them; the years had molded the tissue, but not removed the marks. The nightmares started rising, but, before they grabbed him again, he rolled his old clothes and his belt into a lump, and then threw them into the trash can.

He poured out the contents of his schoolbag.

He didn't need the textbooks anymore; nor did he need his notebooks turned yellow. He found the tickets of him and Maude for the rock concert at the Zenith, and the memories of that event on his way to see her returned afresh. He hadn't heard from Maude since that incident at the periphery of Paris. He packed all this old stuff in his schoolbag again, and then threw the bag into the garbage bin. He changed into the clothes of the warden, slung his duffle bag and the jacket over his shoulder, and emerged from the cabin into the cloakroom.

The guard avowed, in those clothes, Arnault looked more handsome than her boss.

The cloakroom clerk placed Arnault's pay slip over the counter. He explained the wages and the taxes levied, had Arnault sign the papers, and then handed him the pay in cash. Arnault realized he would need time to get used to calculating in euro.

At the exit, the armed sentinel took the release order from the guard. He asked Arnault to state his full name and date of birth. Then he rose from his stool, turned his back toward them, and walked toward a control panel with buttons of multiple colors.

The guard took a deep breath. The paved courtyard with its lights dimmed waited in eerie silence. Then the carriage door grunted and groaned. A crack appeared where its two panels met. The wind from outside widened the crack and rushed in with forgotten smells. The lights from the street flooded in and filled the courtyard with shades of colors.

Arnault bowed to the guard; she squeezed her lips and looked away.

Arnault crossed the street then stood on the bank of the Seine.

On the far side, new homes took the place of old fields. The damp April air from the far bank brought with it the scents of burning wood, reeds and algae, and the chatters of migratory birds disoriented in their nests after a long haul flight.

Along this bank, where the late snow had thawed into slush, daisies and daffodils raised their heads, stretched their stems to the streetlights, and swayed to the chill of a reviving breeze. Arnault's face and armpits sweated. The generous air honed the rank odor that lingered on his clothes. He lowered his duffle bag to the ground, opened the jacket from the warden, and let the heat stagnant in his blood ventilate through his pores.

The bell from the chapel behind peeled twelve times. Arnault closed his jacket, picked up his bag, and headed south along the bank of the Seine. Far out, the lights of Montmartre gleamed over its hill. No public transport ran at this hour. The skyscrapers rose from the shadows in the valley, flanked the hill's silhouette, and showed the long way he had to go.

The embankment sloped down to a concrete pavement. Farther down the road, he saw the shelter for the homeless mentioned by the warden. No one queued before the shelter's gate, but worn out tents lined both sides of its walkway. Clans of men and women stood along the road, drank, smoked, and talked. Each group became silent and watched Arnault approach; he nodded at them and moved on without stopping.

Past the last bridge of this town, the lights came fewer. The concrete bank gave way to a mud trail along the river, closer to the water and lined by ferns. The long barges, carrying sand, debris, and cars, hummed and ploughed through the dark; wakes from the passing boats lapped along this shore, and whirlpools coiled among its tangles of roots. The edge of a tent peeked through the drooping branches of a weeping willow. Arnault slowed his steps and sidled away from the trail to avoid waking the tenant.

More tents surfaced along his way. Near the northern edge of the city, these tents appeared in groups, separated by wooden crates and barrels that marked their territories. He couldn't recall seeing so many homeless in the open before. The smokestack of the factory where his parents worked rose against the pale sky, but no smoke emerged from it now. He wondered about his parents, but his feet didn't let him stop to think about them.

A night train lumbered away over the Seine, rattling the trestle of the bridge. He took the footpath along the canal for ships, skirted the large warehouses that still stood in their places, went before the old sports complex cramped among new buildings now, then stepped on the road that turned into a busy thoroughfare and brought him to his part of the town.

He didn't recognize anything here.

In the place of the covered market, a chain supermarket stood with cameras warning along its front. A new parking lot took the place of the old square. At its lonesome edges, the spared solitary trees whispered about the busy crowd that used to mill around here at all hours. Arnault sought the wooden benches he knew from before, but they were gone now. He didn't belong to this place anymore; this place no longer belonged to him; by following his feet without thinking, he had ended up in the place he wanted to avoid the most.

He retraced his steps to the thoroughfare and continued in the direction of south. He passed before the hotel of Maude's parents and noticed its name was different. He crossed the street of his parents without looking in their alley. The air smelt stuffy around this place, and the noises here didn't come from people. A couple of times, he felt tempted to ride one of these new buses that rolled all night long, but this journey on foot suited him better. He had walked for five hours already. He wasn't far from the heart of the city, and he knew it would be filled with people there.

On the hill of Montmartre, the dawn broke with its first lights. Arnault stood on the stairs of Sacré-Coeur and watched the city sleeping below. A single light shone through the panoramic pane of a penthouse above the public garden and revealed the tents pitched on its patches of grass. A few souls roamed the paved road in front of the basilica and asked for spare changes; Arnault reached into his pocket and gave them money.

He descended the hill of Montmartre through the streets of Pigalle, passed the Trinity Church, and stopped at the square of Gare Saint Lazare. The first passengers rushed into the station or waited on the square. Nobody stared at him here. He bought a coffee then strolled among the travelers who waited with their bags; it was important to get used to being with so many people at once. The road that went up toward Place de Clichy had a couple of hotels that looked affordable, but Arnault didn't feel like staying inside a room or sleeping on a bed. Besides, a state ID, more than twenty years old, wouldn't get him into any of these hotels.

His means were limited too; he needed to find a job before his money ran out. This city was being demolished and rebuilt perpetually. With his workshop trainings and his hands-on experiences in prison, he would find work in one of these construction sites, but he had to be careful about spending his money till then.

But finding a job requires a valid ID. And a valid ID requires a valid address, with proofs to justify at least three months' residency. These were the rules, and his sudden release hadn't prepared him for these rules. But there were helps from the state in such matters; he would have to be patient until he found a decent place to live. There were several shelters for the homeless around the city; one or two allowed longer stays; his expired ID and the letter of release would get him into one of those. With these two official documents, he might even be able to use the shelter's address to renew his ID before three months.

He was no longer near Gare Saint Lazare. His feet had moved on without his knowledge and now he skirted the railings around the church at Madeleine. The gold tip of the obelisk rose above Place de la Concorde, caught the first rays of the sun, and pitched at him over the wide avenue lined with luxury shops and apartment buildings. He went south along this avenue, crossed the paved square empty at this hour, and headed toward the Seine.

Public works, building bicycle lanes along the Seine, blocked his way. He stopped to ask for work, but the workers here spoke only Eastern European tongues. Their manager knew a few words of French but had no idea who Arnault could speak to for work. Arnault noted the name and the phone number on their trailer, and then walked toward the west of the city along the bank of the Seine.

He passed before Place des Invalides and the National Assembly. The quays here were being rebuilt, and the riverside drive was closed to traffic. Joggers came in a continual flow then went around those who slept on sidewalks under the bridges. A few of these runners stopped at the new fitness area upon the bank, used its modern exercise equipments, and then continued on their ways. The quays looked cleaner and smelt fresher. The tents, pitched among the trees along both banks of the Seine, seemed newer and neater too.

Past the Eiffel Tower he switched bank. The quays here had public works going, and he recognized the logos from his workshop. The machines of the French masonry company dug, hauled, and hulked along the shore; they were run by workers who shouted in all languages other than French. The trailer here bore the same name as the one on Place de la Concorde, and the name didn't belong to this French company. Arnault asked one of the workers for their manager; the man understood nothing and pointed at the trailer.

The door of the trailer stood open. The equipments inside showed the place served for their office; it reeked of hard alcohol and hashish cigarettes. Arnault tapped on the panel of the door then waited. Nobody came. He rapped on the door and poked his head inside. The red-faced manager lifted his eyes, shot a glare at Arnault, and then went back to his work.

Arnault passed the Radio France building, then stopped on a bridge and scanned over the Seine. The sun rose from behind, lit the isle ahead, and revealed the statue at the tip of its tongue. This isle didn't look anything like before; but the statue still held the torch out the same way above its head, for strangers like him.

And the swans still lived there. A few of them had chicks; they were learning to brave the waves that came from the passing boats and rocked the isle's shores. A climber's rope hung from the railing of the bridge. Arnault wore the straps of the duffle bag over his shoulders, swung a leg over the railing, caught the rope, and started climbing down.

His feet touched the synthetic floor. He noticed the pegs on the pile and the exercise equipments in the arena under the bridge; nobody was using those at this moment. He skirted the arena, walked along the shore watching the swans, and reached the tip of the isle. The Statue of Liberty seemed shinier than before. He lowered his bag on the soil, sat with his back against the statue's pedestal, stretched his legs out, and watched the traffic on the bridge.

He had walked for nine hours nonstop; his legs agreed with this rest.

2

The noises behind woke him. From the position of the sun over the train station, Arnault figured he had slept for a couple of hours. A regional express train entered Paris from its southern suburbs and poured out the daily passengers onto the quays. A metro liner picked them up, carried them on the bridge over the Seine, and disappeared into Passy.

The arena behind the Statue of Liberty buzzed with a school group exercising. Arnault slung his duffle bag over the shoulder, watched the corded kids strive on the pegs over the climbing wall, turned around the arena, went under the bridge with the rope hanging from, and headed toward another bridge on the east that crossed over Isle of Swans. Rushed office workers, their eyes glued on cell phones, scurried through retired couples ambling on the tree-lined promenade; they switched side or turned back when they saw Arnault coming their way. He climbed the stairs to the bridge, hesitated between going left and right, then saw more frowning retirees coming from Passy and moving out of his path; he turned back and went toward the busy station on the quay of the Seine.

Outside the station, a team of young volunteers handed out breakfast to the homeless. One of them greeted Arnault, waved him over, and held out a paper bag. Arnault thanked the boy, took the bag and a cup of coffee, then crossed the busy boulevard and went toward a shopping area that looked new. He didn't find a single payphone along his way.

He returned to the group of volunteers and asked the boy where he could find a payphone. The boy's eyes froze on Arnault's beard and duffle bag for a moment. Then he took his cell phone, held it out, and told Arnault he could use it to call whoever he needed. The local number for the public works answered in an Eastern European language. Arnault handed the phone back to the boy, thanked him for his kindness, and went inside the station.

Paper maps were no longer given out at the ticket booths. The young woman at the counter opened a map on her computer and showed him the places he needed to go. Things now worked differently from before; but the way today's youth interacted with people like him seemed different too. Arnault thanked the woman for her help, and she told him to ask others along the way; the boathouse on the east of the city offered long term shelters.

The town hall of each arrondissement renews the state IDs for its residents. Arnault knew this rule, and it hadn't changed. But, the Statue of Liberty on Isle of Swans wasn't a valid address for this renewal; he would have to wait until one of the shelters offered him a place. The employment bureau also handled the relief payments for people in his situation; the clerk stated he would accept Arnault's papers of release and pay from prison, but he could do nothing on their system to help Arnault until he returned with a valid ID and a proof of address. The office of social workers, at the town hall he tried, told him the same. The woman declared he wasn't the only person stranded in this social limbo of today; her office raved and ranted daily to change their rules in this new society of homeless; without a valid address, the unemployed under her aegis stood helpless after losing their homes; none of this made any sense, but she could do nothing about it.

The boathouse with long term stays had a nine months' wait. Six of the short term ones sheltered single parents with children. The seventh one took the homeless like Arnault, but had no place available at the moment; the manager wrote Arnault's name down then asked him to check back in a week or two. He listed a few soup kitchens Arnault could go to and secure at least one warm meal per day. The sun was on its way down over the buildings, and the thought of a warm meal, before it became too late, stirred Arnault's stomach.

The mobile soup kitchen at Les Halles that cooked their foods behind the van was run by the city's homeless and volunteers close to losing their homes. Arnault helped them serve the long queue before the van, then grabbed a portion of the food and joined the group that handled the kitchen. Their young manager had lost his job in public works seven months earlier; then, three months later, his rent-controlled apartment too, to those workers from the east who had taken his job; now he slept on the seats of this van, with his eight years old son, who refused to trade the illusions of this city for the realities of province. The boy seemed to love how the city went on beautifying herself while creating this new breed of homeless.

The manager stated the Great Recession had brought an avalanche of public works on France, to stimulate its economy by giving this beautiful city an extra facelift at the expense of French taxpayers, but the French construction companies always filled those jobs with workers from the parts of the European Union that demanded lower salaries. He had agreed to stay with his son in Paris, because the situation of public works in other French cities wasn't better. Arnault thanked the manager for the meal and then moved on with his bag.

In the Latin Quarter he found the outdoor store he needed. The security guard at the entrance stopped him and stared at his beard. Arnault understood. He took out the paper of his release from prison and showed it to the guard with his expired ID. The guard's cheeks lifted in a smile and he bowed to Arnault in deference.

"Twenty-five years?" the guard said.

"Two less."

"I did a fourth."

"Long ago?"

"They released me last year."

"With this job?"

"No!"

The guard claimed he got lucky; a security chief in the metro connected with his pitch and offered him this work. With terrorism on rise, security guards were on high demand, and most places needed guards who spoke French. Some security companies housed their guards on premises, but they needed a valid state ID for employment. With Arnault's stature and experience in prison, he should have no difficulty finding a job in this city, where security companies were popping up by minutes and struggling to recruit French speakers; the high salaries and the generous benefits offered came from this penury of guards in the market.

Downstairs, in the section for camping, he found the tent, the sleeping bag, the cooking gas, and the utensils he needed. He picked up a frontal lamp then saw these lamps no longer had compartments for batteries; they came with a cable and a jack for computers. The area around the Statue of Liberty was equipped with floodlights; if he wanted, he could sit on the pedestal and read; besides, no public library would lend him books without a valid address and ID. He gathered the remaining items, paid for them at the cashier, then headed upstairs.

The same security guard stopped him at the exit. Arnault understood again. He put down his purchases on the table with their receipt then started opening his duffle bag, but the guard dismissed him with a wave saying he didn't need to see any of this; he wrote his phone number on a slip, gave it to Arnault, and asked to call him after renewing the expired ID.

Arnault thanked him for the favor. The guard assured he wasn't doing any favors to Arnault; for every able person he recruited, his company offered him three thousand euros in bonus. With his recommendation, Arnault wouldn't need to waste his time and energy in finding a place to prepare his cover letter and CV.

His eyes softened at Arnault's supplies for camping and cooking. He pointed to a food bank four blocks down the road where supermarkets from the city donated their unsold goods; if Arnault hurried, he could reach there before the place closed. He shoved a shaving kit in Arnault's hand saying he would fare better with the public without his beard from prison.

The food bank was run by young professionals from the city. One of them was a lawyer who also donated her time to a charitable law society. She gave Arnault her card and asked him to call her if he needed help. Arnault thanked her for the offer, took groceries for the next two days, then noted their hours of operation and left the place.

When he reached Isle of Swans, the sun had sunk under the bridge, but still hung over the horizon of the Seine and lit up the blue of the Statue of Liberty in an orange glow. Except for a lone adult who used the equipments in the exercise arena, this end of the isle was deserted of people; only the water birds trudged up the bank in search of a shelter on the isle for the night. Arnault lowered his bags at the pedestal of the statue then went around scouting for a place to pitch his tent.

He found the place under the bridge facing Passy. Shrubs of berries and wild flowers hid the spot from view. He cleared the bird droppings, the pebbles, and the dried branches, then gathered his belongings from the pedestal and brought them over. The top of the low-roofed tent wasn't visible from the promenade that crossed the isle under its bridges. He fetched water from the fountain near the arena and started cooking his dinner.

He saw the card from the female lawyer. The card reminded him he had to call his lawyer if he wanted to know the reason for his early release. He had met this public defender for the last time twenty-one years ago; he wasn't sure if this man still represented him. He had no idea where the office of this public defender was. Even if he knew, he couldn't reach this man without accessing a phone; since that act of terrorism at Bataclan, each cell phone required to be registered with a valid ID and an address. With the payphones replaced by cell phones, he couldn't think of another place to make his calls from; he couldn't go around asking people to lend him their cell phones.

The thought of a lawyer brought back other thoughts too: his desperate pleas for innocence; the stunned jury returning a guilty verdict nevertheless; the gendarmes taking him from the court; the van of the penitentiary driving him away from Paris along the Seine… He didn't want to go any farther back. He was out of that nightmare now. He adjusted the flame of his burner and stirred the spaghetti sticking at the bottom of his pan.

A swan couple settled with their chick for the night at the bottom of this sloping bank. The parents sat down on the grass, but the chick preened its grayish feathers, lifted its neck in between grooming, and checked what Arnault was doing before his tent. The chick's innocent gestures showed no fear or mistrust for him. The parents didn't look scared either, but they kept their vigilant eyes on the chick.

Suddenly, Arnault missed the prison and its people. After all those years in that cell, this place in the open felt too spacious. The vast amount of air that the Seine brought over its current to this isle suffocated him.

Throughout the day, his dealings with people had kept the feelings out, but now, with the sun gone for the day and the darkness falling upon the river, this long isle, open on all sides, was closing upon him. This family of swans kept one door open, and he chose to use that door to reenter life.

He needed to feel at ease with the present to call this spot on the isle his home.

He pushed aside what lay in the past, what was no longer real, and decided to live in the present. But the present didn't feel real. He forced himself to find an anchor in the present by touching what he had at this moment. He cleaned the tent that was already clean. He rearranged his stuff in the duffle bag. Then he sat down and counted his money.

The security guard from the outdoor store returned to his mind. With all other avenues closed, searching for a job in the public transport was the way to go. These twenty-three years behind the bars hadn't been a total waste; he had come away with valuable skills. Luck doesn't fall from the sky into your hands; you've to do your part to strike upon it. He knew this rule. The cold and the unknown didn't daunt him. This place under the bridge offered him the shelter to eat and sleep. He accepted this grace from above with gratitude. Then he decided to devote his time and energy to search for a job. That was far more important than calling the public defender and discovering the reason for his early release.

His food was ready. He switched off the burner and let his spaghetti cool. Night was covering the Seine. He felt dirty from moving about all these places for all these hours since his release. He undressed, entered the river, and swam against the current.

The cold took his blues, the efforts toned him.

He climbed up the bank, dried himself, and changed into the clean clothes he had picked up from a charity.

He didn't feel hungry yet. The swimming had given him the pitch to search for a job in public transport, but he also needed a silent pitch during his moments of rest. He flattened the cardboard wrap of his utensils, took out a pen from his bag, and headed toward the Statue of Liberty. He sat on its pedestal and wrote under its light:

'Man without shelter, looking for a job.'

3

The daily passengers and the tourists returning from Versailles filled the compartments close to the turnstiles to their limits. The next regional express train to Paris was marked cancelled due to the ongoing strike. The one after wouldn't come before an hour and forty-five minutes. For their urgent meeting this morning, she was already running late by twenty minutes. Lucy went farther down the platform, chose one compartment that still had some breathing space left, and sent a text message to Marc apologizing for her delay. These frequent strikes were becoming the other problem of living with her parents outside Paris.

A reply came from Marc immediately saying he understood. He reminded her to check the details on pages forty-six and fifty-eight of the indictment file he had emailed her last night. He asked her to be extra careful on the train with this highly confidential document.

There was no privacy in this compartment. Lucy found a tiny space near the condemned toilet where others wouldn't look over her shoulder, opened the document sent over to her firm by the side of prosecution, and started rereading the charges listed on the two pages mentioned by Marc. The remaining pieces of the puzzle fell to their places and a clearer picture of their scheme emerged before her eyes; she smiled at their thwarted brilliance.

The alarm sounded. Just before the doors closed, a homeless man entered the compartment and stood in front of her with his back to the toilet. Lucy ignored him and went back to reading the rest of the indictment.

But the presence of this homeless man bothered her.

She lifted her eyes from the file and checked the man from the corner of her eyes. He posed no threats to her confidentiality; he didn't even look at her; but the way he held his trunk and head put her ill at ease. His face and eyes announced a recent loss of home, and he didn't seem comfortable with so many people compressed into such a small place. She closed her file then read the cardboard sign the man held at his side; the letters on the sign, crafted with care, didn't come from an uneducated mind.

The man sensed her uneasy stare; he gave her a subtle bow then moved away.

He greeted the passengers and then started his pitch. His clear diction and resonant voice turned many heads, but then his stature—and his number of years in prison—cleared people away from his path. He finished his speech, went to the far end of the lower floor, then returned by the upper floor to her end and stood by the door holding the cardboard banner in front of him.

'Man without shelter, looking for a job.'

A few passengers came forward and offered him money, but he refused their offers with a polite calm saying he was looking for work only.

At the next station, the man descended from the train and left behind a deep silence that reigned over the compartment. Lucy opened her file again, but the words from the man's sign kept crawling over her pages. A woman standing next to her sighed and said, in these days of economic turbulence, she too could become homeless in matters of moments.

Lucy reached her station in Paris and descended from the train. She searched around the platform, but didn't see the man anywhere; he must have continued with the train. She wondered how many homeowners would trust a homeless man, released after twenty-three years in prison, to enter their home and do repair works. She took the footbridge over the rail tracks, zigzagged through the cars jamming and honking on the boulevard by the Seine, ran on the bridge over Isle of Swans, and reached her law firm in Passy.

Marc had left a pile of documents on her desk with a note: there was no point in her coming to the meeting now; he would stop by at the end and brief her on the proceedings; if she could sift through this pile and pick out a few more arguments for the defense, he would appreciate her help.

Lucy blushed.

She couldn't stop the warmth rising in her for this young, handsome partner—gallant, intelligent, and kind. She pushed her feelings aside and plunged into the documents.

The plot was ordinary, but the players weren't. Their modes of operation rivaled high-octane espionage series on television. The screen company had used seven layers of opacity in transferring the money from the dictator and the bank's investors to the construction company mandated to build the factory for producing weapons of bio-terrorism. Lucy searched further on this screen company, but its details were blacked out everywhere on the indictment sheets; for some reason, the four partners of her firm wanted to keep those details confidential among themselves. She opened a fresh document on her computer and started listing the points in favor of the two French companies hung on the pegs of justice.

The bids and the works of the construction company seemed legal; they wouldn't stay on the penal hook, except for their use of illegal labor. The problem was with the bank. The attorney of the state had nailed them with laundering the dictator's money and financing terrorism using investors' funds; other than the hemorrhages in the financial market, caused by the sanctions imposed on this bank from the USA, she couldn't think of other points for their defense. The indictment stated the payments had passed through this Central American screen company, but she was clueless about how these payments connected the two French companies with this dictator on the African continent; the layers involved in the transfer were hidden from her eyes, along with the details of the screen company.

Marc entered her office then closed the door.

Lucy rose from her chair.

Marc squinted on the document on her terminal, then went around her desk and stood behind her. His breath on the nape of her neck raised her hair and tickled her face. He kissed her lobe, whispered the words she loved in her ear, then left her and went to the front.

She told him the difficulties she was having with this case. Marc's face darkened for a moment, but then his poised smile returned.

He assured her she was barely a month away from her partnership in this firm, she would have access to all their confidential documents thereafter, and, until then, he had enough to keep her busy over their long weekends coming. He took two unsealed envelops out of his jacket, left them on her desk with a wink, and then went out the door.

The tickets were for Corsica, for the first long weekend of May. The hotel stood on a cliff by the Mediterranean, in Porto Vecchio. The name on Marc's folder caught her eyes. Her face tingled again, but not for the same reason; he must have left this confidential file behind by mistake. She picked up the file and rushed toward his office before it became too late.

4

Someone pulled the zipper of his tent.

Arnault lifted his head from the back and watched the entrance. A long neck entered through the slit in the flap, and the eyes of the swan chick surveyed the content of his tent. Arnault reached out and opened the rest of the flap; the chick went back to its parents, then stood there and watched him from distance.

Arnault came out of his tent and stretched his limbs. The dark before the dawn reigned over the isle, but its first rays lit the slate roofs on both sides of the Seine. He closed the flap of his tent then went toward the exercise arena to work his muscles; the ropes, the pegs, and the equipments here anchored him in a routine he knew; with all other structures gone, these small bits, known to him, were important to start another unknown day.

Since he settled on Isle of Swans at the beginning of April, two and a half weeks had passed. Since then, he had also omitted his past in prison from his pitch, but the rest of his speech didn't gain him more than a few looks of pity; the passengers who used the public transport didn't have the means to offer him employment, and the security guards with their muzzled dogs confirmed their companies needed a valid ID to work for them. His earnings from prison were running out; he didn't want to ask for money from people without working for them; he would have to enlarge his perimeters in and around this city to find work, but the tickets for public transport in Greater Paris came expensive.

A crayfish, freshly killed, lay in front of his tent. An adult swan, the larger of the two parents, went down the slope in unhurried steps. Arnault moved back and stood away from his tent, but the swan showed no intention of returning and fetching its catch; it reached the other adult and the chick at the bottom of the bank, and then sat next to them. Arnault rubbed his face, returned to the crayfish, and picked it up in his hands.

He opened the flap of his tent and brought his cooking utensils out. He fetched water from the fountain, lit his gas burner, and let the crayfish boil. He cut carrots and zucchinis, sliced tomatoes, put a part of these vegetables on a lid, added the spaghetti left over from last night, then took the filled lid to the swans and placed it before them as usual.

The chick wobbled to the lid then gabbled over the food. Arnault peeled the boiled crayfish, ate it with his loaf of bread and a portion of the raw vegetables, and watched the rising sun bathe the Statue of Liberty on the western tip of the isle.

At the station, he bought a day-pass for the city, and then took the packed tram that went around the periphery of Paris; the strikes of public transport no longer paralyzed this city or angered its citizens. He continued his pitch with a renewed vigor, refused the monies and thanked their givers, reached the end of the line, descended from the tram, then took another tramline and continued along the city's periphery.

He reached the terminus. What he saw around this place slowed his steps and changed his mind about going any farther.

Since the Arab Spring, refugees from the African continent had flooded the countries of Europe. He had seen them on the streets of Paris, struggling to cope with the unforeseen, but he couldn't believe what his eyes were seeing now at this margin of the city: the camp extended all the way to the border of the Seine and held refugees of all ages—some younger than a year, and others older than eighty. A few lived in beaten down and worn out tents; most took the generous sky for their cover; in between them, through the cramped spaces, tireless volunteers went on distributing bags of food, boxes of clothes, and other supplies.

A family of six, camping in the tunnel, tried to stop their two younger children from crying by offering them food, but these children seemed anything but hungry. A young woman from this family, elegant and erect, blushed at Arnault, then took the two children in her arms and tried to calm them by whispering in their ears.

Arnault saw the Zenith across the river and froze in his place.

He recognized the spot too; only its occupants were different. He recognized the neighborhood that didn't look anything like before. He recalled the moment from twenty-four years ago, about the same time of the year, but at the end of the day. He strived not to close his eyes, but the slain woman with her throat slit, his fight with the three vagrant boys, the blow at the back of his head, and the fading noises from the dying woman—all these images from before rushed in and blurred out what he was seeing before his eyes now. He wiped his face and forehead; he forced his feet to move on from the spot; he crossed the tunnel under the overpass and continued down the sidewalk toward the circular road at the periphery.

The storage companies still operated here at this periphery. The movers' vans went in and out of their premises. Only a few men stood by the circular road. Arnault joined the queue and waited for his turn. He didn't have to stand long. The wages, higher than what he had earned in prison, came in cash. And he didn't need a valid ID or address for this job.

5

Lucy left her office then waited for Marc on the bridge over Isle of Swans.

After she saw that screen company's details on Marc's folder four weeks ago, the case was taken from her and given to another associate in the firm; she was surprised to see his lack of trust in her. Their trip to Corsica was cancelled. Since then, rumors had circulated in the corridors, and the four partners had become tense with all employees of the firm. Last week, investigators raided their offices without notice and carried away loads of documents with them. Marc had refused to say a word to her about what was happening to their firm, but, for an instructing judge to be present like this during search and seizure was a rare event.

The sun was dropping behind the Statue of Liberty when Marc appeared on the far end of the bridge. Lucy strained her eyes, but his gait showed no anxiety after this meeting with the other three partners of their firm. Marc reached her and watched over the Seine. Then they took the stairs down and descended on the promenade across the isle. They walked side by side, in silence; Marc didn't try putting his arm around her. Lucy saw the single women go by and give Marc the eye, but, this time, he didn't notice any of them.

That screen company in Central America was all over the press this week. Lucy hoped Marc wasn't tangled with this company's affairs in any ways. Unlike the other three partners, Marc had come from a poor suburb of Paris and worked his way up through the system; she didn't want to see him ruined by this scandal. She wondered if Marc, as the youngest partner of their firm, had been tricked into dealing with this Central American company somehow; from what she knew of him, she couldn't see him getting involved in this mess on his own. Like these other partners,

Marc too considered money important for their firm, but she respected him for the way he kept his head on the shoulders.

They reached the western end of the isle, climbed the stairs, and stood in front of the station for the regional express trains.

"Is everything alright with your flat now?" Marc asked.

"Not yet."

"How are the repairs going?"

"Coming along."

"Will they finish soon?"

"No."

Marc admitted he understood her plight. Over his years at the law school in Paris, he too had lived the same nightmare of commuting daily from the suburb through strikes. He reached out, touched her cheek, and apologized for his recent ways with her; he offered he would be delighted to have her over to his place for the night.

Lucy hesitated, but then agreed. She sent a text message to her mother. The two of them crossed the busy boulevard and Lucy stopped in front of the ATM to withdraw money. Marc stood at a distance and busied himself with his cell phone.

Lucy was about to punch in her code, when a shadow appeared to her left, and one more to her right. She pressed the cancel button and hurried to recover her card. A hand from the right snatched the card before her and put it back into the slot. Another hand from the left grabbed her by the throat and pressed her forehead against the top of the ATM panel.

Lucy wrenched her neck off then screamed.

A sharp point pressed against her lower back. A coarse voice ordered her in broken French to punch the code for her card.

Arnault heard the scream on his way out of the station. He saw two vagrants pinning a woman against an ATM at knifepoint. Her companion, a fit man in sleek suits, tucked his phone away in the satchel, turned his back toward her, and fled from the scene.

Arnault dashed through the stalled cars.

With a blow to the temple, he sent the unarmed attacker reeling to the ground, and then grabbed the other attacker's wrist that held the knife. The scuffle began. He tripped over the first attacker who sprawled on the pavement and lost his balance.

Lucy shouted again for help, but saw Marc nowhere.

Passersby stopped on their tracks then came running; drivers left their vehicles and rushed over. The two fighting men fell to the road. Her attacker still held on to the knife, but his wrist was pinned to the pavement by her rescuer on top. She crushed the attacker's fingers with the sole of her shoe until the knife came off his hand. She kicked the knife aside then took out her phone, but another woman was already calling the emergency.

With the knife gone, the fight didn't last long. Her rescuer rose from the road, watched the motionless attacker on the pavement, then folded his arms over the chest and stood aside; blood seeped from his face and forehead where the skin showed scarped. The other attacker hadn't moved since he fell to the ground at the beginning of the fight.

A screaming police car reached the scene. An officer took the pulses of the two attackers on the pavement then called the paramedics. The other officer took Lucy's statement, then lifted the knife from the road and placed it inside an evidence bag. The paramedics came and drove the two immobile attackers away from the scene.

An officer asked her rescuer for his ID and address. The man gave his name then said he lived under a bridge over Isle of swans and he didn't have a valid ID. A flash of this homeless man crossed before Lucy's eyes but she couldn't recall where she had seen him before. The officer took the man's expired ID and called into his station. Lucy noted her rescuer's features and tried to place him among the homeless men she had come across this week, but then realized, since this turmoil started rocking her law firm six weeks ago, she hadn't paid attention to anyone.

The officer finished his call then turned toward Lucy.

"We're taking him to the commissariat."

"For the fight?"

"No."

"Then why?"

"He has a record."

The officer avowed he admired what Arnault had done for her, but the police procedure required to book him for public disorder; with the testimonies from her and others, Arnault should have no problem getting out by tomorrow. The officer shook her hand, then patted Arnault on the shoulder and led him toward their car without cuffing his wrists.

Lucy watched the police vehicle leave, then gathered her purse from a bystander and headed toward the train station.

A female voice called her from above.

A woman stood at an open window over the ATM. She held her phone out and declared she had filmed the entire event. Lucy confirmed she wanted the video. The woman gave her the flat number and asked her to come up.

Lucy went to the door and buzzed her intercom.

6

The sting on her lower back woke Lucy. She checked the time on her phone; if she left home within forty-five minutes, she could catch the first train to Paris.

The dots around Arnault had connected over the night; she needed to check a couple of points on him to make sure; if she hurried before the workday started for the city, she might be able to find what she needed. She showered quietly, disinfected the knife wound on her back, wondered if Arnault's face and forehead had been treated since the paramedics dressed his wounds last evening, put on her work clothes, then left a note for her parents and rushed toward the station.

A thought occurred to her along the way. She stopped to make sure she had her law license with her. A homeless man stopped and held his hand out; she greeted him, put a bill in his hand, and ran into the station. The first regional express train from Paris reached its terminus and unloaded its groups of tourists who filed toward the turnstiles marked 'Chateau de Versailles.' Lucy waited for them to pass, entered the train, then sat at a solitary corner and replayed the video from the woman.

Her train stopped at the Javel station.

Outside, she paused for a moment and stared at the ATM on the other side of the boulevard; contacting the bank would add nothing more to the video from the woman above, as the police already had her two attackers in the custody; she hoped they hadn't died since the paramedics took them. She bought a coffee from the vendor, let its caffeine thaw the chill coming over her, then gathered her courage and descended the stairs that plunged into the darkness of Isle of Swans.

She found nothing under this bridge. Arnault had told the police he lived under the bridge, but four bridges crossed over Isle of Swans. The other three bridges had no one living under them either; the posh neighborhoods on both sides of the isle would never allow any homeless to camp here. Yet, for Arnault to surface around the Javel station, he had to live somewhere on this isle; unless, of course, the police had already sent their people and fetched his belongings for evidence. The nascent rays of the emerging sun threw patches of rainbow colors on the western end of the isle and painted the Statue of Liberty in green; the swallows searching for flying insects pierced through the dark and dispersed its shades that resisted the approach of the dawn. Lucy went under the last bridge of the isle, crossed the exercise arena, then sat on the statue's pedestal and rehearsed her strategy for Arnault.

She heard the childish rasps and honks. She saw the swan chick pulling on the flap of a tent behind the pile; thick bushes and undergrowths hid the rest of the tent from her view. She lifted her purse then went toward the tent, but two adult swans raised their wings and trumpeted at her. She stopped. The swan couple and their chick observed her for a while, and then calmed down. She stepped closer, found what she needed to confirm, photographed it for the police too, then stood away from the tent and observed the place around.

She smiled at the three vigils of Arnault.

The officer-in-charge informed her that Arnault was in a single cell and would be interrogated this morning. Last night, after booking him at the station, they took him to the hospital for his wounds, and, today, after his interrogation, he would return there for a follow-up visit.

The officer also confirmed they hadn't called a public defender for Arnault yet, but if Lucy wanted to represent him, that could possibly be arranged. He picked up his phone, talked to the head of his station, and then passed the handset to Lucy.

The captain admitted it was unusual for the victim of an aggression to represent the saver, but, given Lucy seemed stable, and given her role at the commissariat was limited to assuring the rules of fair interrogation, he was allowing her to represent Arnault. Subsequent to their report of interrogation, if the prosecutor decided to transfer Arnault over to the depot and present him before a judge, Lucy would have to obtain a special permission from the tribunal of Paris to keep representing Arnault.

She thanked the captain then handed the phone back to the officer.

The officer confided, off the record, his boss was a good man turned pessimist from what he saw everyday. Her two attackers, revived and booked, had confessed to the crime. If he were in the place of Arnault last night, these two men would have left with something worse. Being a lawyer, she certainly knew that nothing was ever to be taken for granted in criminal law, but the wisdom of his cynical boss was to be reserved for the worst case scenario. He took Lucy's license number, had her sign the papers for representing Arnault, and then granted her access to all the legal documents pertinent to this case.

Lucy enquired about Arnault's former record.

The officer stated Arnault's previous conviction dated from twenty-three years ago. His online access to the details of a case was limited to fifteen years back. On his system, he could see only the following elements: Arnault was convicted for a first-degree murder; he had always claimed his innocence since; on the second of April this year, the justice released him unconditionally, because the existing evidences no longer sufficed to hold him in prison. An association of lawyers had fought for Arnault's release; if Lucy wanted to know more about his case, she would have to contact this association.

A murderer of first degree!

Lucy saw she was clutching the edge of her skirt. She recalled Arnault's pitch on the train from Versailles, and the reactions of the passengers to his speech; she wondered what kind of a criminal would go about announcing his number of years in prison.

But then, on that day, in that train from Versailles, Arnault didn't seem like he was boasting about his term in prison. He stated the facts, in a neutral tone, and asked for a job. He mentioned in details the skills he had learnt in the workshops of prison, but he didn't vaunt his skills. And he had the dignity to refuse, in all civility, the money people offered him from pity. If he were a murderer with uncontrollable rage, he would have killed these two men who had attacked her; he had the stature, the strength, and the skills for the kill.

That reminded her of the video from the woman and the photo of his cardboard sign. She handed both to the officer and confirmed she had nothing more to ask about Arnault's case for now. The officer registered the two elements then went out to fetch Arnault.

The hours passed after Arnault's interrogation. Lucy used the time to file the police report of her aggression with the social security, and then with the complementary health insurance provided by her employer. That entitled her to ten days' paid leave of absence.

She thought of calling her law firm and informing her secretary, but then she figured Marc might have informed the office already, and the partners had other headaches bigger than her absence to deal with for the moment. She wrote an email to the managing partner, attached the leave of absence granted by the social security, and then copied the email to Marc and her secretary. She didn't hear back from anyone in her firm.

Shortly after noon, the officer-in-charge informed her that Arnault had returned from the hospital to his cell, but there was no news from the prosecutors' office yet; given the number of cases that went per hour to that office from all the commissariats in Paris, this delay wasn't a surprise for him. He asked if he could get a sandwich for her on his way back, but Lucy thanked him saying she wasn't feeling particularly hungry.

After the lunch hour, she called the association that had fought for Arnault's liberation. The president of the association regretted that Arnault had returned to the hands of justice this soon; she wished Lucy good luck then passed the call over to the lawyer connected to Arnault's case. Lucy gave this lawyer the basics of Arnault's situation at hand then made an appointment to see her the following week at the association's office. She also called the bureau of public defenders at the tribunal of Paris and found out who she had to contact for a special permission, in case she needed to represent Arnault beyond today.

The afternoon gave into evening. There was no news about Arnault's release. The officer-in-charge sent a fax over to the prosecutors' office then asked Lucy to go back home and wait to hear from him. He had her number; he would call her as soon as he had any news. Lucy insisted on staying at the commissariat unless it became a problem for them. On his way out of the commissariat, the officer led Lucy to their conference room and allowed her to rest on the couch. Fifteen minutes later, a bag of warm food and hot coffee arrived for her from outside the commissariat, all paid by someone. Lucy sent the bag to Arnault in his cell, then took out her phone and dialed her mother's number.

The call went answered at the first ring.

"Are you done at the commissariat?"

"No," Lucy said. "I won't be home tonight."

"Do you really have to stay there?"

"Yes."

"Your father is a lawyer too."

"So?"

"You must be crazy not to sleep in your bed."

"Dad said that?"

"Yes."

"Tell him this: The man who risked his life for me would sleep tonight on the bunk of his cell."

"That isn't worse than sleeping in a tent."

"Mom!"

"Do you need us to bring anything over?"

"No."

"Are you alright?"

"Yes."

"We worry about you."

"Don't."

"Call us if you need anything."

"I won't."

Lucy threw her phone on the sofa, closed her eyes, and clutched her hair. She wondered if Arnault, too, had parents somewhere, and if he had taken to the streets by his choice. Suddenly, she missed her apartment in Paris.

The ringing phone woke her up. The officer-in-charge informed her that Arnault was on his way up from the cell. Lucy blinked several times then stared at the digits on her phone: ten past four in the morning. She rubbed her face, arranged her hair and clothes, then sat upright; there wasn't time to go to the washroom and freshen up for their meeting.

Arnault entered the room alone then stood near the door. Lucy noticed the fresh bandages on his head and on the sides of his face. She rose from the sofa and started going toward him, but then stopped when Arnault lifted his hand; his injured middle finger of the right hand was now braced with a splint.

She fumbled for words, but her tongue failed on her.

For the first time it occurred to Lucy she had never thanked Arnault for saving her. When she mentioned this, he assured her she had done far more by defending him. When she offered him money for a hotel, he thanked her for this kindness, and then refused her offer saying he had performed only an act of civility; he wasn't accepting any monetary or other rewards for this.

Besides, he wasn't a man without shelter anymore.

He had a home of his own.

7

When Arnault reached Isle of Swans, the sun was barely rising above the bridge over the Seine and setting the two bell towers over Notre Dame on fire. A church bell rang six times from the side of Passy and drowned the drones of the vehicles that cleaned the streets at this hour. He stood on the bridge at the eastern end of the isle. He watched the water of the Seine coil under the bridges and flow into the dark that lingered along the bends of the river. Then he took the stairs down to the isle and headed west along the tree-lined promenade.

The cleaners collected the trash from the bins and replaced their transparent plastic bags. The early joggers passed by without looking at him or staring at his bandages. Those exercising at the arena moved out of his way and changed machines. He reached the Statue of Liberty then sat at its pedestal and watched the slivers of the sun caught in the rolling folds of the turgid water. With the splint on his finger, no movers would hire him for day labor; he would have to find other means to sustain himself until his finger healed.

The trip to this commissariat, however, had solved the most vital issue.

The charity that collected the mails for the homeless and served as their legal address for all official matters wasn't far from this commissariat; the officer-in-charge knew the ex-convict-turned-priest who ran this charity; once Arnault filed the necessary papers at the city hall of this arrondissement, the officer would pull his strings at the prefecture and get his ID renewed within a week. He didn't recall the police treating detainees this way before.

He checked the address of this charity and their opening hours. He would have time for a wash and change of clothes before their doors opened. He rose from the pedestal and then went toward his tent.

The tent wasn't there.

Nor any of his other belongings. The brushes around lay trimmed to the ground. The three swans sat on his spot and guarded it from intruders. The chick rose, wobbled over to him, and pecked around his knees. Arnault bent over and patted the chick on its back; the two parents pointed their bills to the sky and trumpeted in turns. Arnault went over and crouched before them; the two adults lowered their necks, then sat down and observed his face.

Beads of sweat trickled down his forehead and dripped on his thigh. The sides of his ribs became wet too. Arnault rubbed his face and stood up to go. The chick came stumbling after him and then stood before his feet. Arnault stopped, caressed the chick's head, then pushed it back toward its parents and turned away from this family of swans.

The rasps and the trumpets rose behind him again.

Arnault covered his ears and forced his feet not to retrace their steps. Past the exercise arena, he removed his hands from the ears, sprinted along the promenade, and dashed up the stairs; he didn't care if people stared at him or rushed away from his path in fear.

On the top landing of the staircase, he stopped to breathe. The bondage had come off him; he was free again. Halfway down the bridge, an impulse gripped him and tried to turn his head toward the isle, but he kept his eyes ahead and forced his feet going. He reached the end of the bridge, ignored the volunteers calling him for breakfast and coffee, bought a ticket from the machine, then crossed the jammed boulevard and rushed into the tram about to leave.

The moving tram thawed his blues. At the city university, a group of students entered his compartment and asked the passengers to sign a petition. One boy started talking to Arnault about social changes he had never heard of in prison. Their conversation explained the open attitude of the youth today. He descended with this group of students before the terminus, shared a coffee with them at a roadside stall, and then continued his journey toward the periphery of Paris. Along the way he remembered he had to go to that charity and obtain a proof of address for renewing his ID, but he had the whole day ahead of him for doing all these formalities; after spending forty-two quiet hours in that cell at the commissariat, he wanted to walk around, observe the movements of life, and talk to people again.

He reached the terminus at the periphery of Paris. The vehicles of volunteer groups, charities, and humanitarian associations helping the migrants from the African continent jammed the major artery and the side roads; Arnault didn't want to get in the way of their service. He skirted the congregation of citizens and migrants, reached a row of walled out buildings that looked like abandoned warehouses of a factory, and continued toward the bank of the Seine. The vans of movers grabbed the day laborers queuing along the circular road on the periphery then drove off in different directions of the city. Around the corner, at a solitary spot facing the woods, a ladder leaned against the wall and passed people over.

The people passed over the wall were women: both adult and underage. All of them came from the migrants' camp.

Farther down the wall, in front of a narrow gap, aged bourgeois men, with smiles from various degrees of comfort and complaisance pasted on their faces, queued patiently for their turns and avoided each other's eyes. The group of vagrants operating this ring noticed Arnault. They stared at his bandages and clothes. Then they discarded him for a potential client. Arnault felt his jaws stiffening and fists clenching. He turned his back to the wall, crossed the woods, then took another way and went back toward the migrants' camp.

He reached the tunnel under the overpass, but the place didn't bring back his nightmares this time; the clamors and confusions that rose from the sidewalks cramped with refugees removed all thoughts from his mind. None had tent in this place; the wide overpass served for their cover. Arnault wanted to save his money until the splint came off his finger. At the mouth of the tunnel, he found a spot large enough to fit one person. From a vehicle that distributed supplies to these refugees, he fetched a blanket and a bedspread, then claimed the vacant spot and sat with his back against the tunnel's wall.

He recognized the refugee family from his previous trip here. The young African woman, who had blushed at him last time, stared at his bandages now, but the emotions radiating from her eyes didn't show fear. The rest of her family turned to look at him too. She whispered in the ear of the older boy, then poured hot drink from a pan into a cup and nudged him with her elbow. The boy brought the cup over to Arnault and placed it before him.

Arnault stared at the pale coffee then picked up the cup.

8

The law office was put on hold till further notice from the department of justice. Everyone connected to the case was restricted from traveling outside Paris or talking to anyone else about the case. The investigators obtained permission from the judge then combed through their email server. After two long interviews, conducted over her medical leave, they let Lucy off the hook and asked her to stay away from all personal communications with Marc for the moment. The four partners were told to get their lawyers and appear before the judge separately. The chief executives of the French bank and the French construction company were called as witnesses to the case for the time being. An official request was sent to the Central American government for the records of transactions from the screen company.

The regional express train stopped at the Saint Michel station. Lucy took the bridge over the Seine, crossed Isle of the City, and reached the office of the association that had handled Arnault's release.

The lawyer in charge of Arnault's dossier received her at the entrance then led her to their conference room. The walls of this room were lined with Jeanne d'Arc facing the sacrificial pyre of logs with smile, Marie Olympe de Gouges standing fearless at the feet of the scaffold, a frowning Victor Hugo scratching the back of his head in front of the faculty of law at the University of Paris, and an unflinching Marianne waving the French flag over men fallen at her feet in Liberty Guiding People. Lucy thanked this woman for rescheduling their meeting then sat down at the table across her.

The lawyer gave Lucy the basic details of Arnault's case.

"The DNA test released Arnault," the lawyer said. "They found no trace of his DNA on the slain woman. Before dying, she put up quite a fight. It would have been impossible for Arnault to attack this woman without leaving his DNA on her."

"DNA test existed back then," Lucy said. "Why wasn't it used for his trial?"

"No idea," the woman said. "The defense didn't call for it probably."

"What's keeping Arnault from being declared innocent?"

"Potential complicity."

"Pardon?"

"The DNA strain found on the victim was also found on Arnault."

"How many strains did they find on Arnault?"

"Three."

"That fits his statement."

"It does."

"They found no matches for these three strains in their database?"

"Not yet."

The woman stated the DNA test couldn't declare Arnault as innocent, but it had instilled sufficient doubts in the eyes of justice for not holding him in detention any further. Restoring Arnault to innocence would require a separate trial with a new jury, and that trial could only be arranged if the DNA found on the victim linked someone else to the crime. Unfortunately, that DNA didn't match any strain; not just in France, but also in the entire European judicial database. Until now, the owner of that DNA had never been booked by the police for a crime anywhere in Europe; they had no other option but to wait.

Lucy asked this woman what had pushed her to fight for Arnault's release.

The woman confided it was Arnault's pleas for innocence. Those weren't just any pleas; they were backed by facts and matched by evidence. She had heard about the case, read about it in the press, while she was still a law student. The association had plenty of cases on their desk, but she chose this particular one for its elements. Like Lucy, she too was surprised to discover how the procedures for Arnault's trial had been conducted; particularly, the absence of DNA testing. When she pressed for the test, no trace of Arnault's DNA was found on the victim. She could then use this fact for his immediate and unconditional release.

Personally, the woman confessed, her hunch came from a ring recovered from the scene of crime. She saw some vagrants in France use those rings to trick people into giving them money; she, herself, had been tricked by them a couple of times in Paris and Lyon. But most of them were harmless rovers who earned living for themselves and for their families by playing inoffensive tricks on the unwary and the naïve; they rarely attacked people. She had heard of Lucy's misfortune near the Javel station and of Arnault's bravery to save her. The incident resembled what Arnault had encountered twenty-four years ago when he was tied to this woman slain at the periphery of Paris. The ring recovered from the scene carried the same DNA as the club that had been used to clout Arnault at the back of his head.

A clan of vagrants lived in those days at the periphery, but, the woman admitted, she had no clues to whether this particular clan had records for committing violent crimes. Several gangs of criminals lived in the underworld of Paris. Each gang's mode of operation depended on its chief's disposition and the pressure exerted on its members to earn money. Arnault and this slain woman had fallen victim to a gang particularly violent, but it didn't necessarily imply these three criminals had come from that clan of vagrants at the periphery; they could have come from other parts of Paris or from anywhere else. The proximity of the Zenith made that area a paradise for the night clubbers and the night stalkers.

The woman added that the procedures for Arnault's liberation hadn't required her to meet him in person, but, given the facts of the case, she believed what had happened at the scene of the crime was the following: Arnault saw the three men mugging this unlucky woman, got into a fight with them, and received the blow that left him unconscious. The muggers, instead of slaying Arnault, then set him up with the knife they had used to slit the woman's throat. If they had killed Arnault too, the police would have known the truth and searched for the culprit of the double homicide; by leaving Arnault unconscious with the knife, the murderers had escaped the police.

All these theories, the woman emphasized, came from her intuitions only; none of these had any importance at this moment; if the authorities could tie someone to the unmatched DNA one day, it would be a different matter. Until then, Arnault would remain tainted with doubts in the eyes of justice. It was unfortunate that the victim Arnault had tried to save wasn't there to testify in his favor, and that lieu at the periphery of Paris had been deserted at the time of this crime.

Lucy asked if she could join the association and work on Arnault's case with her.

The woman mentioned she had heard of the scandal around Lucy's law firm. She had no problem letting Lucy in, but she would need to check with the other two executives of the association. Concerning Arnault's dossier with the justice, nothing more could be done for the moment, except for waiting and hoping that the real perpetrator would turn up with the unmatched DNA in the police database somewhere, but if Lucy personally wanted to represent Arnault before the justice, she should join the bureau of public defenders at the tribunal of Paris and get Arnault to sign the papers for his representation. The head of that bureau was a former classmate of hers; she, too, had left the money for the law; if Lucy wanted, she could go over there now and talk to her about joining her team.

Lucy thanked this woman then went to the bureau of public defenders.

The head lawyer of the bureau received Lucy in her office; her friend from the association had already called her about this. She warned Lucy of the low pay for this job and the risks of being called in the middle of the night to represent detainees before the instructing judges. She didn't care about the legal storm-head building over Lucy's law firm, because the investigators had already cleared her out of its range. Lucy could start as soon as she wanted; with the number of crimes rising in the streets of Paris, the bureau desperately needed more lawyers. Lucy gave her license number and personal details to this woman, then took the forms for representing Arnault and left for Isle of Swans.

Arnault's place under the bridge lay clear. A fresh red sign, crafted in white letters, declared camping as illegal in public places and referred to the relevant code of law. Lucy called the commissariat. The officer-in-charge confirmed they hadn't touched anything on that isle; Arnault might have picked up his stuff from there and moved on to some other place; the homeless often did that to avoid the eyes of the city. The officer informed he had asked Arnault to call if he needed help to renew his ID, but Arnault hadn't called the commissariat so far, and they hadn't heard anything about Arnault since his release.

The red sign told Lucy something else.

She went over to the municipality and asked the department in charge of cleaning the isle. She was told the dirty stuff of the vagrant had been dumped into their trash. The photos she had of Arnault's spot and his belongings showed no dirt on them or around his tent.

Lucy placed her law license before the manager.

On her phone, she showed him the code of law that prohibited them from discarding the personal belongings of others, without holding those in Lost & Found for a minimum duration. She also showed him the penalties for violating this law.

The manager's face darkened. He scratched his head and pulled his beard. Then he went away for several minutes and returned with Arnault's stuff. Lucy thanked the manager, gathered Arnault's stuff in her arms, and left their building.

She wasn't going back to her parents' home with Arnault's belongings. She crossed the bridge over the isle, reached the Javel station, then continued down Rue Emile Zola toward her apartment; she hadn't been there for seven weeks since that thunderstorm. She ignored the residents who stared at Arnault's stuff in her arms. She emptied her full mailbox, avoided the elevator, and took the stairs. She removed the chaos and the debris left by the repairers on the landing in front of her apartment. She turned the key in the lock, forced the jammed door open, and entered her flat condemned by the damages from the storm.

She was shocked by the state of her flat. Tools and materials lay strewn everywhere, punctuated by empty beer bottles and crushed cigarette butts; the stale odor confirmed her place hadn't seen its repairers for two weeks at least. The broken window pane stood gaping in the den and invited the late spring showers and the hungry pigeons to enter her apartment. Lucy put down Arnault's stuff at a corner away from the damaged window, then sat on the molded sofa and took a stock of the place; she had difficulty recognizing her flat.

Yet, it was her place.

She had paid for this flat with twelve years of her salary; nobody could take it away from her; she didn't have to follow anyone's rules in this place. She hadn't slept here for seven long weeks; yet, in spite of the mess here, she felt connected to this flat. She couldn't imagine how she would react, if someday she returned here and discovered her flat emptied out or occupied by someone; or, found her building torn down and leveled to the ground.

A tent is the only home a homeless person has; how awful it must feel to return to your spot and find your place of security gone. Lucy hoped Arnault had moved on to some other place and found other means to build a new home. In a city of so many homeless and homeowners, she would never see Arnault again.

The thought of building a new home reminded her of something else. She stood up and moved away from the couch. She recalled the part of Arnault's pitch in the regional express train about his skills in home repair; they matched his statements at the commissariat about his workshop trainings in prison. She remembered his values from their exchanges in that conference room at the commissariat after his release. With her tongue tied before him then, she had struggled to help him without hurting his dignity and feelings. The solution to all those problems now lay in front of her, right before her eyes, inside her apartment.

Given the delays of their repair works and the state the repairers had left her flat in, any sensible homeowner would cancel their contract. Given what she had seen of Arnault and heard from him, she could trust the repair of her apartment in his hands.

She only had to locate Arnault and offer him this job.

9

The swallows at the mouth of the tunnel woke Arnault. Since this route was closed to traffic, these birds had nested in the cracks on the cornices and the façades; the break of dawn was the busiest time for the adults to feed their chicks with mosquitoes. East of the circular road, the top tiers of the steel and glass towers caught the saffron rays of the dawn and sent them over to this camp to wake up and stir its people. Dawn was also the feeding time for the migrants who left this camp during the day for their labor.

Zala brought the breakfast over to Arnault. He bowed to her then asked if Isayas had returned last night. The young African woman turned her head to the side and stated in her firm, lucid diction that this was the third time her brother hadn't returned home at night, and his gradual change was beginning to worry her and their parents.

Arnault confirmed the boy wasn't made for the heavy physical work of these movers, but he was intelligent and, with a bit of trying and a stroke of luck, he might be able to find some other work that suited him better. Zala asserted their father had no trouble with this physical work; Isayas had always sought the easy ways out as far as she knew; and, along those ways, his superior intelligence would get him someday in troubles.

Arnault assured her that the boy had already picked up a decent vocabulary in French; in a few more weeks, he would be able to supervise the day laborers from this camp who worked for the movers. He would talk to Isayas about this, but, in the meantime, if Zala could keep her brother away from the hands of these thieves, it would be good for their family.

Zala regretted she couldn't keep Isayas from these thieves because they were all over this camp recruiting people.

Arnault finished his breakfast then left his spot. The vans of movers were already going in and out of their warehouses; with the splint taken off his finger last week, he was happy to return to work with the able boys and men from this camp.

Like Zala's family, most of these migrants were genuine refugees. They had fled the terrorist acts of that African dictator and risked their lives in crossing over to Europe for the basic necessities of survival. They made sincere efforts to learn every word of French he was teaching them. Their day labor, of high quality and paid in cash, was a winning deal for both the movers and the migrants. With his ID renewed now, he could have taken a job with a security company, but he loved living in this camp and working with these migrants.

He would have to find a way to build sense into this young Isayas's head.

He found Isayas at the limits of the woods. The traffickers were already busy passing the human merchandise for their clients over the ladder. Arnault grabbed Isayas by the wrist and took him away from the wall. The boy tried to wrench his wrist off and run, but Arnault didn't let him go.

"What do you think you're doing?" Arnault asked.

"Watching."

"Watching what?"

"What they're doing."

"Do you know what they're doing?"

"Yes."

"Then why are you watching?"

"Just curious."

"Would you like this to happen to your sister and mother?"

"No."

"Then go away and work!"

Arnault followed Isayas and made sure the boy crossed the camp, joined his father, and filed with the others toward the periphery for day labor. He had difficulty understanding how Isayas, coming from a family like theirs, could turn out so different from the rest. The way Zala had cared for his broken finger and wounds showed the boy didn't lack affection in this family; his own parents and relatives hadn't cared a fraction of this for him.

Both parents of Isayas took their turns to work and guard his younger siblings. His sister Zala cleaned homes and hotels daily. The boy had to understand how one derives dignity from honest work. Watching the ways of these traffickers or stalking the streets of Paris with their thieves wouldn't get him an inch closer to understanding this truth.

The predators were already on their prowl in the camp. Their stout chief did his rounds with the usual gang and marked out their feeds: the girls and the women to be sent over their ladder; the kids, the old, and the handicapped to be shipped out to the popular parts of Paris for begging; the boys and the men to be recruited for stealing. This migrants' camp at the periphery, sprawling over six blocks already, had become another source of living for this clan of exploiters who occupied these abandoned warehouses of the closed factory illegally. There was nothing he could do to stop them from exploiting these migrants, but they needed insiders to tip them on potential exploits; he hoped Isayas wouldn't betray his own people by collaborating with them.

The chief of the clan noticed Arnault and gave him the glares.

Arnault turned his back toward the man and walked toward the movers' vans picking up the day laborers on the circular road.

There was no point in his clashing with these predators. They couldn't prevent him form doing what he did for these migrants. More and more associations were coming forward to help this camp. More of these hard-working migrants were being accommodated in different parts of France that required their manual labor. He just had to make sure this chief and his clan wouldn't coerce those refugees who had chosen honest ways out of their plights; he could do little for those migrants like Isayas who fell for temptations and lures.

The authorities certainly knew what was happening at this periphery. He couldn't be the only person to notice the illegal activities carried out by these traffickers using the migrants from this camp. Plenty of associations, humanitarian agencies, and individuals came here daily to help these migrants. He hoped Isayas wouldn't end up provoking a disaster for himself or for his family someday. He hoped the authorities would take measures to stop these racketeers here before it became too late.

10

The contractual notice of three months disappeared with the suspension of her law firm. The creation of this screen company in Central America was pinned down to Marc, along with the payments in and out of that company: to the account of the African dictator, and to the account of the French constructor, both held at the French bank; and to the offshore accounts of all four partners, for the counseling and legal services provided by their firm.

Because of the exodus of adults from that country in Africa, the French construction company, with help from this African dictator, had used child labor for building a part of the factory that produced his biotechnological weapons of war. The French law now pursued its citizens for crimes committed on children outside France. If the investigators tied the executives of this French construction company to the exploitation of these children in Africa under dangerous conditions, for manufacturing weapons of mass destruction, they wouldn't see the light of freedom for too long.

The investors who had trusted the French bank with their monies were now suing the bank for using their funds to finance terrorism. The lawsuits in the US alone totaled over two billion dollars. The American authorities barred the French bank from all transactions on their soil. The French legislature rushed to pass new laws to deal with the corruptions of this order; the French justice struggled to apply the existing laws in capturing this new breed of criminals; and the officers of the French executive branch lost their sleep over how to keep this reeling bank from succumbing to the financial shock and triggering another crisis for their nation that was just raising its head over the wakes of the Great Recession.

The public gave up watching their favorite series on television. What they were getting from these real actors, in real time play of real actions and events, turned out to be far more exciting than what they usually got from their favored series as fiction.

Lucy used the time between her two jobs to search for Arnault.

She visited all the shelters in and outside Paris. She asked all the homeless groups that slept on the streets, on the platforms of metro, and under the bridges. She visited all the soup kitchens, the dispensaries, the associations, the charities, and the humanitarian agencies that served the homeless and the poor. Nobody had seen Arnault or heard of him anywhere.

Over time, she came to see that the homeless lived in clans to survive. One clan had little or no information about another. Or, if they did, it was for the competition of survival. For her, Arnault didn't seem like someone who would belong to any of these clans. And in the parallel worlds of the homeless and the homeowners, except for rare occasional crossovers, a member of one world had no clues about members from the other; they didn't even see themselves as belonging to the same species.

The laws of jungle applied in this forest of humans.

With the passage of time, she came to think Arnault might have traded the cold of Paris for a warmer region of France, but then he didn't come across to her as someone who would be affected by cold weather or the coldness from people.

Over time, she also came to see other truths about the homeless. They drink to stay warm and keep realities out of their lives. They sleep more than others because they have nothing else to do. They sleep during the day because, at night, they're chased out of the warm places, and they have to keep moving to stay warm. The problem of a homeless isn't one of shelter and hunger alone; it's also of loneliness in a world flooded with humans.

In the jungle, an animal finds security in its lair. The world of the homeless is constantly in flux. The belongings of a homeless are kicked around and thrown about nonstop. For a homeless man, the spot he sleeps on, the stuff he carries with him, the places he draws his sustenance from—these constitute his home really; he feels no differently from a homeowner from losing these. After roaming in the homeless world for three weeks, she couldn't see these people in the same light as before.

On a night of torrential rain in July, Lucy noticed, from the window of her room at her parents' home in Versailles, someone shivering at a bus stop across the street. The man had been there for two weeks already: a recent homeless, always lost in his thoughts, sitting on the bench with his elbows on the knees and his eyes on the ground, ignoring the passersby and all else happening around him; he never asked for help or got in anyone's way.

On this particular night, he paced inside the bus stop to stay warm and kept hugging his arms around the torso. He noticed Lucy at the window and stopped to look at her. The emotions on his face echoed sorrow and self-pity. Lucy went down with two blankets and gave those to the man. When she asked what had brought him to the streets, the man threw her gifts to the garbage and walked away from the bus stop into the rain without a word.

Three days later, the man was discovered dead on the stoops of someone's home.

With her neighbors, Lucy organized the man's funeral and paid for its costs, but the experience left her in a deep void, filled only by painful wisdoms: Most homeless, in their past, grew up at homes. They had parents, relatives, and friends who gave them warmth and love. The homeowners like her, when they meet a homeless man, they want to know his past, more out of curiosity than compassion; or, from the fear that the same misfortune may fall upon them. And most homeless don't want to talk about their past, because it throws them back into their regrets, resentments, and nostalgia for the good days behind them; these make their homelessness harsher to bear. They want to talk about their present and the events of the society. They, too, are citizens with their rights to vote, their rights to privacy, and their rights to opinion about the world and its state of affairs. They find it ruthless when others pry into their past and consider it appropriate because they're homeless. What you can't do with a homeowner, you can't do with a homeless either.

Lucy started with the bureau of public defenders and with the association of lawyers that had liberated Arnault. For the first time since graduation, she felt she was doing the job of a real lawyer, and not shadowing for an elite law firm that used her brain to skirt the rules.

She no longer cared about the money. She was the sole legatee of her wealthy parents; she had a roof over her head and her basic needs fulfilled; if she didn't apply the laws she had spent five years in learning, she would grow old with a sense of irreparable impotency. The thrill of her two new jobs drained her sometimes, but she continued her search for Arnault on the side and over the weekends.

The scandal around her former employer continued to grow. She became more and more aware of the plights of the African refugees who had fled from the terrors of their dictator to the dangers and privations on the streets of Paris; she no longer looked at them with the same eyes. Among these people, some with money might have faked documents and paid their way to Europe, but most were genuine refugees struggling to cope with the nightmares they had escaped from and the nightmares they were facing in this unknown city. Their dignity prevented them from asking for help from the civilians of a country whose government was straining to its limit to grant them asylum.

Every family, stranded on the street with their children, hungry and scared, tugged at the salaries and the bonuses she had drawn from that law firm in Passy. She started buying foods and clothes, and giving those to the families that refused her money.

She saw the predators that prowled the streets and stalked these refugees. She saw their females harassed by the pimps. She saw their males coaxed or coerced into tricking and stealing. She saw the worn out vans pick up the children, the old, and the handicapped, and then dump them at the metro stations for begging. She also saw most refugees resisting these racketeers with civility and dignity; only a few lost their heads and fell into these rings.

One night, she was called to defend a migrant African boy for stealing. Before the instructing judge, the boy confessed he was a recruit of the clan of vagrants that lived at the periphery of Paris, and he stole because he wanted to feed his hungry family. The judge shook his head then let the boy go with a stern warning.

After she moved back to her apartment in Paris, she had a lot more time to herself. The unfinished repair works in her flat kept her out on the streets most of the day and night. For the first time in her life, she came to see how beautiful this city was, how its beauty shifted over the hours and through the weeks, how each arrondissement of this city added a unique charm and twist to its beauty; she vowed never to live outside Paris again.

In course of one of these walks, she discovered a unique enterprise in the heart of Paris. It was created by some volunteers to accommodate the local artisans and workers who had lost their jobs from the French construction company that now used cheap labor from the eastern states of the European Union. She went inside their workshop hoping to find Arnault there, but they had never seen him or heard of him.

She took their details and kept those for Arnault. If she could locate him one day, this enterprise had exactly what he needed for work.

11

He combed through the migrants' camp at La Chapelle. He searched all the streets around the camp. He asked all the volunteers, the associations, and the humanitarian agencies that helped the migrants here. He found no traces of Isayas anywhere.

The boy had taken the judge's grace as a sign of encouraging his actions; he was going farther and farther away from his family and getting involved in more and more dangerous dealings. Arnault left the quarters of La Chapelle and headed east under the overpass of metro; he had promised Zala to bring her brother back before this evening.

He reached Stalingrad. He checked the major camp of refugees on the main square; then the minor ones around the quarter too; he didn't find Isayas at any of these places. He found the same chief and a dozen of his men haggling with the migrants around this camp. The chief saw him too, then held his stare and glowered. Unlike the camp at the periphery, where Arnault's people kept these prowlers at bay, here they had a full reign over the entire territory; Arnault could do nothing about it.

He left these predators to whatever they were doing with the migrants here and went on with what he had to do to fulfill his promise to Zala.

Isayas's association with vagrants was bringing security threats for the women like Zala. These young women from Africa were far more beautiful, healthier, and dignified than the women the racketeers had in their hovels at the site of the old factory. These African women fetched a lot more money for the traffickers than their own women and children did. And the old bourgeois perverts who used the services of these pimps didn't want the smell of this roving clan on their skins.

Zala's elegance and beauty stood out among her people.

So far, she had been lucky with the cleaning works she found. But with Isayas's progressive involvement with these traffickers, the rich perverts were approaching her more often and asking for her service at their homes. Until now, Zala and her parents had seen through their disguise, but Arnault wasn't sure for how long she would find this camp a safe place to live. He had reached out to several humanitarian agencies for them, but all housing facilities for refugees in France now had waiting lists more than a thousand people long, and, with winter still five months away, nobody was rushing to get these refugees into homes.

Arnault arrived at Bastille. He searched the popular spots where thieves target tourists. He repeated his search at Place de la Republique. He still didn't see Isayas anywhere or find any information about him. He took the canal, reached the quays of the Seine, and headed in the direction of Notre Dame; he knew the malls and the shops along this way that served as fertile patches for vagrants and thieves who targeted particularly summer tourists. Isayas wasn't at any of these places.

Arnault heard the commotion and stopped.

He followed the eyes of the bystanders and looked upward. He saw a child hanging from the balcony of the top floor apartment; the windows and the balconies on both sides of the child had no one. Heat rose to his head and pumped through his muscles. Before he knew, his shoulders had pushed through the crowd, his feet had leaped, his hands had gripped the lower bar of the first balcony, and they kept reaching for the upper rails one after another.

Roars of applauds rose from below.

Arnault's hands and feet went on working like machines. On the third floor, a child burst out laughing then sprayed him with colors. On the seventh floor, a woman screamed and slammed the door of her flat. Her scream brought the neighbors out on their balconies. A tattooed man emerged with a stout club in his hands, saw Arnault on the ninth floor and the child hanging two floors above, and started encouraging both. The panicked child turned his head to the side and revealed the top of his T-shirt caught on the railing. Arnault positioned himself directly below, kept his eyes on the boy, and went on working his hands and feet.

He reached the eleventh floor and lifted the boy onto the balcony.

The media replayed the event over and over. Lucy saw it, heard it, read about it a thousand times; yet, each time, a new part of her reacted to the event. They buzzed about the child and his mother; they buzzed about the criminal record of this crazy rescuer covered in wild colors; they buzzed about his home at the migrants' camp on the margin of Paris.

By mid-afternoon, the video of the bystander had gone viral over the net across the world and fetched ninety million applauds for the heroic act of Arnault.

An impulse seized Lucy.

But she knew how to resist. The child's mother—a single woman, unemployed over two years—had gone for a job interview, leaving her son alone at home, and then been delayed by more than two hours. She was being held in the custody of police, and the child had been placed in the hands of social workers. If this woman didn't have money to hire a babysitter for her son of six years, Lucy doubted she would have the money to hire a lawyer for herself. After what the boy had lived this morning, he needed his mother at his side, and Lucy saw a better way to compliment Arnault by complementing his action; he would certainly appreciate this act of hers far more than her charging at him with praises.

Lucy called the commissariat where the child's mother was being held.

12

The media vans left finally. Arnault sighed in relief and went on with his life at the camp. He found Isayas at a den of thieves, dragged him back to the camp, and put him at the feet of Zala. He forbade the rebellious boy from leaving the perimeters of the camp and put him to watching his two younger siblings while his parents and older sister went out to work.

Then one dawn, before the men left for their day labor, a fleet of armored vehicles left the circular road at the periphery and approached the migrants' camp in a single file. The words soon spread through the camp and raised panic among the migrants. The city had dismantled two other camps and dispatched their refugees to various parts of France, at times separating members of the same family. The people who lived under this overpass had built a sense of community and a life of relative comfort among them; with their works paid in cash, they didn't want to leave this shelter and security behind.

The migrants looked up to Arnault and saw, like them, he too was frowning at the approaching vehicles.

But the vehicles didn't enter the camp.

To Arnault, these vehicles didn't look like the ones the authorities used to dismantle a camp or destroy a barricade; he didn't see any bulldozers among this fleet of vehicles. A troupe of armed guardsmen descended from the vans at the front, entered the camp, and marched in measured steps toward the tunnel, without looking at anyone; they seemed to know where they were going.

Arnault saw that the marching band belonged to the National Guards of France. They entered the tunnel, passed the refugees on the sidewalks as if they didn't exist, ignored the gaping mouth and eyes of

Zala, scouted him out among the migrants, and halted a few yards away from the group he was standing with.

Arnault left the group and stepped forward.

The guardsman at the front separated from the column, stopped in front of Arnault, and gave him a military salute. Arnault bowed in return then offered his hand to shake, but the guardsman didn't offer his.

"Monsieur, please come with us," the guardsman said.

"Where?"

"We're not allowed to say."

"With my stuff?"

"No."

"Is this an official order?"

"It's a request, Monsieur."

"From whom?"

"We can't say."

Arnault realized he was being moved to a shelter for the homeless. The publicities around the rescue had put him in the spotlight; the authorities couldn't leave him camping illegally under this overpass. When he requested them to protect these refugees from their predators who preyed on them daily, the guardsman stated his rank wasn't commissioned to handle that mandate; he was strictly following what he had been asked to do.

Arnault bade goodbye to the family of Zala and others he knew at the camp. He regretted he might not see them again; they should continue the way they had started, but without him. He asked Isayas to consider the ways of honesty and diligence, if he wanted out of his plight with dignity someday. He avoided Zala's eyes because he knew what he would see in them. All through his rounds around the camp, the armed guardsmen stayed at his side with deference; they didn't rush him in any ways.

This was different from his former experiences with the law.

They escorted Arnault to their vehicle. This wasn't a van that belonged to the penitentiary of France; it was a vehicle of the National Guards that bore the French flag and the emblems of its military glory. They sat him in an expensive leather seat at the back of the van then fastened the seatbelt for him.

The van moved.

The fleet of vehicles left the quarter and reached the circular road at the periphery. Arnault strained his neck at the camp below. The residents stood in a file at the limit of the camp and watched the vehicles go above them; he didn't see Zala among these people. Little by little, the campsite disappeared from his view. Once more, he was giving up a home he had known for three months, to find his shelter in some place unknown.

The fleet entered the city from north. Arnault recognized the route he had taken on the day he was liberated from prison. The vehicles went over the cemetery of Montmartre, passed Park Monceau, continued on Avenue Wagram, and reached the Champs Elysées.

Goosebumps covered Arnault's forearms.

A delegate received him at the palace and escorted him to a room for rest. He was requested to shower and change into new clothes. The shirt, the suits, and the shoes were made to fit his size. He was told his belongings were being kept at a safe place; if he wanted, he could recover those after his meeting.

The president didn't waste his words on Arnault.

He stated he wouldn't lower Arnault's act by clichéd praises. Instead, he was offering Arnault a job that matched his strength and courage. The French Republique honored its glory by offering this job to Arnault.

Arnault was free to accept or reject it.

13

The authorities listened to his request.

About a week after his meeting with the president, the camp of vagrants at the periphery went dismantled. Bulldozers tore the walls down, leveled their hovels to the ground, and recovered the closed factory and its old warehouses from their grip. Several of them were arrested for vagrancy then placed at the feet of justice. The associations that defended the rights of vagrants stayed out of these operations because they knew this particular clan to be notorious for their vicious exploitations and violent crimes.

A construction company Arnault knew of demolished the closed factory and the surrounding sheds in the simmering heat of August. Then, as the parched city regained its colors through autumn, the buds of new buildings sprouted from these ruins and raised their nascent heads over the periphery.

A new life emerged at the place that had lain dead for half a century.

For some reason unknown to Arnault, the construction company decided to use the labor of the migrants who camped at the periphery. Over the summer, a few went dispatched to other parts of France, but most found employment with this constructor and made this quarter they knew their lieu of asylum. The government rushed in and legalized their papers. The construction company brought over their mobile homes and trailers. The migrants left their spots in the camp and moved into their new homes at the site of construction.

Zala's family was given one of the bigger trailers.

Her father found work at the construction site, but not her brother

Isayas. Zala continued to clean homes and hotels, but, with her papers legalized, she now found work through a cleaning company in Paris; they gave her all the social covers that came with a regular job. Her two younger siblings started school in September. She and Arnault kept pushing Isayas to study or work, but the boy refused both routes.

Isayas's progressive involvement with the outlaws singled him out from the migrants who ran out of patience with him; he became a delegate of the chief of vagrants who, after their expulsion from the site of the old factory, settled into the woods across the river.

In all parts of France, the law designated places for travelers. Most traveling groups limited themselves to these places and respected the laws that governed their stays. This woodland, at the margin of Paris, wasn't one among these designated places, but this clan of vagrants, after the warehouses were taken from them, took it as their legal right to stay on this spot. They had lived and bred at this periphery for decades; these quarters belonged to them; their chief and his assistants terrorized other traveling groups that stayed at the designated places nearby, but those groups reached out to the authorities and pushed their oppressors back. The laws, however, couldn't dislodge this violent clan from the woods.

With most males from the migrants' camp now absorbed into heavy construction works, their unguarded females and children were left to be poached; this clan of truants, bandits, and marauders targeted and exploited them with a renewed vigor.

And, this time, their vigor also came with a smell of vengeance.

Contrary to his apprehensions, the new life at the barrack suited Arnault. Driving their vehicles to the sites of drills, running with his colleagues in Paris and in the surrounding woods, jumping off the bridges into the Seine and pulling the dummies out—he was honing skills that fitted his make, in the company of rescuers as devoted as he was; this line of work excited and absorbed him far more than what he had learnt in the prison's workshops.

The migrants didn't fade from his mind.

But, with the rising intensity and responsibility of his trainings, Arnault found little time for his old friends. And these migrants too, drawn into the climbing demands of the new constructions, found little energy left for any social meetings. They didn't forget their former mentor, but now his national acclaim established a barrier between them and kept raising it as time eroded. Once more, Arnault had to let his past go and flow with the present; his new colleagues provided him the anchor he needed.

On the day of their national festival, Arnault distributed calendars on the streets of Paris and at people's homes from door to door. This furnished a new entry into the civic society that had kept him out for a quarter of a century. Those citizens who recognized him from his rescue clips had his signature drawn on their cheeks and on the hollows of their throats, next to the tricolor marks. That evening, the ball of rescuers drew a number of Parisians the squad had never seen before. Arnault stayed with them until the break of dawn and danced to the tunes of songs he had never heard of. At one point he saw the female lawyer from the commissariat standing in the crowd at the front, but the continuous file of dancers on the platform left him no time to go and talk to her.

The donations collected by their squad this year exceeded all records.

Little by little, Arnault forgot everything else and plunged into the codes of the trade. He learnt them quickly. The mandatory training period limited his assignments at first, but his common sense and poised patience gave him an edge over others. The captain of his squad accelerated his training and, before the end of that summer, he passed all the tests and obtained his certificate of autonomy. The squad rewarded him with a month-long course in mountain rescue conducted by their special branch in the Alps; Arnault saw the mountains for the first time in his life.

Then, in the beginning of October, he received his first real call of emergency.

14

The press rallied the job the president offered to Arnault; her reserved pride boiled. She marveled over Arnault's poised steps at the rescuers' ball, but he didn't come over and ask her to dance. Lucy knew, with the demands from his new job, Arnault wouldn't have time to repair her flat; she used the services of that enterprise she had located for him in Paris.

The scorching summer eased into a soothing autumn, but not for everyone. The reports from Central America confirmed Marc's signatory authority over the screen company. The financial records showed, on behalf of the African dictator, he had signed off money to a terrorist organization that targeted American officials in that country. The American authorities demanded his extradition, but the French justice told them to wait until Marc finished his required terms in France for assisting a foreign dictator in committing crimes against humanity, helping a French company to employ children in dangerous works, and laundering money for terrorists using the services of a French bank.

The CEO of the French bank, under fire from all sides, screamed for help, got none from anyone, and threatened to lay off three thousand employees in France. This threat got him the attention his bank needed from the government. The French officials, in spite of the public howling, bailed the bank out with taxpayers' money and started a polemic all over the country. The authorities responded by arresting the CEO of this bank and placing him on the altar of justice.

The arrest didn't calm the frenzied citizens in France. They argued, instead of preserving the guillotine in a museum for souvenir from the years of terror, and, instead of lodging this CEO in a luxurious prison then feeding him with more public money for several decades, the government should bring the guillotine out under the sun, sharpen and shine its blade, oil its rails, and then use it on the neck of this crook at a public square. While the justice fought the defense team of multimillion euros put up by this bank, the public cooled their anger off by punishing its CEO in their dreams.

The French construction company, on legal hook for exploiting children in Africa to produce weapons of terror for a dictator, took a different route to soften the eyes of justice. They wanted to remedy a part of the damage caused by their actions to these migrants in their home country. The constructor offered to employ these migrants and furnish them with lodges during their work, if the government went ahead and legalized their asylum.

The government rushed to collaborate with this construction company.

The free movements of labor across the EU had marginalized many French workers and pushed them out of certain jobs by their low salaries. These workers had moved on to other professions and no longer wanted to return to jobs that failed to earn their livings with dignity. The Great Recession had revealed the vulnerability of non-uniform nations subject to uniform economic laws across the EU. The nationals, who had worked for less before, now demanded more, because the salaries in their home countries had risen from the drainage of labor. While the legislators rushed to patch up the situation by passing new labor laws across the EU, the French jobs that required heavy labor saw no one coming to them.

With thousands of refugees seeking shelter and manual work all over France, and, with this French construction company pleading to employ and lodge them for repentance, the government saw the solution for both sides in a single move that also saved public money; they legalized these refugees and gave them permissions to work.

The city then granted this construction company permits to demolish the old factory and its warehouses at the periphery and raise new buildings in their places. These works needed heavy machineries that only a giant like this French constructor could have. The city also made life easier for them by dismantling the camp of vagrants that lived on this site and perpetrated their crimes with impunity. This pleased the citizens because, for decades, the abandoned site had become the breeding ground for vicious and violent acts.

The labor for these demolition and construction works came from the migrants who lived on that edge of Paris. They had the will to work, but lacked the skills for western norms. The French constructor lodged them in the trailers and mobile homes that were waiting for new residents since the departure of their Eastern European occupants to their home countries. The few French employees who had remained with this company after its African scandal were put into training and supervising this new workforce of migrants.

The constructor, with its labor force renewed and fresh permits issued, attacked the old site with a new frenzy. The place was torn down and dug out in two weeks. Within six more, the first pillars of the new buildings rose over the periphery and met its hot, thick air.

Lucy came to know about the arrests at the periphery of Paris.

She reached out to the commissariat in that jurisdiction, told the officer-in-charge she worked for the association that had arranged for Arnault's liberation and was handling his case now, and then obtained the results of the DNA test done on these men; none of them matched the strains of DNA still hanging in limbo in Arnault's dossier. With little to do on this case until fresh elements turned up, she pushed Arnault's case to the back of her mind and focused on her two new jobs, but the strategy for his new trial, running at the back of her head, brought one thought to the front.

The arrests made from that clan at the periphery had brought only males in their twenties and thirties. This was coherent with her research that showed these clans used their younger males for violent works and kept the older ones for chores less demanding. If those who committed the crime twenty-four years ago had been in their twenties and thirties then, they would be in their mid forties and fifties today. The fact that the DNA strains in limbo from Arnault's dossier didn't match any of these arrested men's wasn't a surprise.

Lack of light hid the attackers from Arnault at the time of that crime, but, since then, other elements connected to the case had confirmed their ages.

She recalled her discussion with the colleague who had fought for Arnault's release. A clan of vagrants lived at the periphery at the time of that crime, but there was no guarantee the criminals who committed the crime had come from this particular clan that lived illegally on the site of this old factory. They could have come from any place in Paris or from anywhere else, committed the crime, and then moved on.

According to her research, at the time of that crime, several gangs lived around the limits of Paris. Since then, the expansion of the city, the renovation of its periphery, and the construction of the circular tramlines had pushed these gangs farther out into the suburbs or brought them closer into the heart of the city; those limits today boasted of apartments and facilities that drew the nouveau rich and kept the poor out. Among the greeneries at these new limits, the law still reserved a few spots for the traveling groups, but those where harmless people who came from different parts of Europe, stayed for a certain length of time, and then moved onto other place. They didn't settle into illegal places and breed their clans, as these vagrants had done at the site of this old factory for over four decades.

Three traveling groups now lived on designated sites around the migrants' quarters at the periphery. Lucy visited the three and met their chiefs; they all seemed decent; her polite refusal to accept their drinks came from her impolite doubts about their hygiene and from her bourgeois education on never accepting anything from the unknown. These legal zones of rest were equipped with electricity, running water, and toilets. And, like other campers, these travelers also used bottles of gas for cooking and heating their caravans and tents.

These traveling groups stayed away from the mainstream. The mainstream society didn't want them either. But they obeyed the society's laws and stayed out of its troubles. Some stayed longer and enrolled their children at schools; others home-schooled their children on the move. They earned their livings by day labor; by removing voluminous appliances and furniture that lawful citizens deposited unlawfully on roadsides and fields; by sifting through the city's debris and collecting the recyclables left by the educated informed in their trash, such as plastic wraps, corks, cardboards, cans, and bottles, and then selling those to recycling plants for a pittance. A number of associations helped these traveling groups and defended their legitimate interests.

When the clan of vagrants, kicked out from the site of the old factory, terrorized these traveling groups and tried to take their places, their chiefs reached out to the law and defended their rights; they didn't yield to these threats, fall into violence, or sacrifice their people.

This clan of vagrants then gave up and settled illegally in the woods.

15

The tram dropped her in the middle of an ethnic market. Stalls lined both sides of the main street and brought back the colors and smells from her trips to Africa with parents in the childhood. Lucy navigated through the chatters and laughs that surrounded each stall, lost her path several times through the islands of people, asked for help and got more than she sought, emerged from the milling crowd, then saw the overpass and sighed with relief.

This was the first time her feet touched the pavements of this quarter in Paris, and her impressions didn't fit the images she had gleaned from the press. The dense crowd of the variant people here didn't threaten her in any ways; on the contrary, it made her feel safer in what she was about to do. She recognized the new constructions over the old warehouses to her right and, by her calculations, she was no more than eight or nine hundred meters from the spot she wanted to visit. She took the sidewalk inside the tunnel under the overpass, saw the remnants from the camp of the migrants who lived on the construction site now, covered her ears and stepped aside when a police car and an ambulance rushed by with their sirens and strobes on, and then reached the woods on the border of the Seine.

She didn't see any vagrants here. She checked the pages of her research; the map showed the clan lived somewhere in these woods.

A bridge crossed over the Seine at this point. The woods continued on the far side bank and, among its trees, columns of smoke rose at regular intervals and met the cloud of exhausts that hung over the circular road jammed with cars, vans, and long-haul vehicles. The booms, the thumps, and the raw rattles came from the construction site behind her and drowned the drones from the barges that plodded through the river with their load of sand, cement, iron, and debris. Nobody took this bridge at this hour, but she wasn't going back after coming this far. She tucked away the pages of her research, took the purse off her shoulder and held it by its straps, then stepped onto the bridge and continued without looking back.

She saw the shacks of crates and boards with chimneys at the top that smoked. She saw the caravans with antennas and satellite disks on their roofs. She saw the washers and dryers that stood outside their hovels, the open toilets that lined this side of the woods, and the drainpipe that disgorged their sewage directly into the Seine. She reached the end of the bridge, then stopped to gather her bearings and collected her thoughts.

She had informed no one before coming. She could have informed no one about what she wanted to do here. She was entering these woods, not an enclosed place; houses lined the far side of this clearing; cars went to and from that hamlet; if she had to, she could run out into the open and shout for help. She saw the cables that took electricity from under the bridge and delivered it to the hovels of these vagrants. A thick black tube of rubber, tapped directly into the line that supplied water to the hamlet over the clearing, carried water to this clan for their daily needs. Lucy wondered if the residents of this hamlet worried about the contamination of their water and called the authorities to fix the problem.

She skirted the woods and found the opening for the clan's vehicles.

Her steps on the mud trail turned a few heads, lifted a few more, and raised alarm only for an elderly woman. Lucy ignored the alarm; she was in her full rights to stroll in these woods. The residents here weren't foreign to seeing aliens from the outside world, but they probably never saw females of her profile daring upon this path or venturing through their hovels. The ill languished in couches lifted from dumpsites; the depressed old lumbered about doing works too onerous for their age; the tired women dragged their feet, did their chores, then stopped and stared at her.

Lucy saw more than just fear and disbelief in their stares. But then, from what she had read about this clan, she wasn't expecting any better. She didn't see the chief of this clan or any of its younger males; they must still be busy with their rounds through the city.

Under an open shed, surrounded by filth, a scared woman in her twenties gave birth on the dirt, assisted by four matriarchs in their middle ages. The hospitals in France guaranteed free care for everyone; Lucy wondered why the chief of this clan prevented this young woman from going to one for her labor.

At a secluded corner, she saw more scared men and women huddled together. She had seen these handicapped men and women strewn over the city for begging. Now she saw the instruments that were used upon them to produce their handicaps. She had read about these unfortunate people too, but she wasn't expecting the gore to be of this order.

Her stomach revolted.

She quickened her steps, passed the remaining shacks and caravans without looking, then stood at an emotionally safe distance and tried to gather her poise and courage. She was only at the beginning of her mission and she hadn't talked to any of these people yet.

A chorus of raucous laughter erupted and jolted her out of the stupor. A gang of rowdy children emerged from a hideout then went chasing each other ignoring her presence. The late afternoon sun sieved through the foliage and lighted the autumn flowers in their hairs and the bands of colors on their ankles and wrists. Those who caught others fell and rolled on the grass; the rest ran in circles and sang their tunes. The ones on the ground didn't stay long either; they finished their romps, rose covered in leaves and dirt, then joined the songs and danced with others. They weren't curious about her or bothered by her watching them.

These children, lively and beautiful, didn't fit their worn-out, worrywart adults; Lucy wondered at what point their metamorphosis occurred. The laws in France required mandatory schooling for children up to a minimum age, but she couldn't see these children in the classroom or courtyard of a school; the scared parents here would never defy their chief by sending these kids to one, or by using the system of national education to school them at home. With no education, these children would stay bound to their clan and pay for the cares they were receiving today from their parents. These adults too had lived the same experience with their parents; as a result, they saw this system of security as normal within their secluded clan. Lucy doubted anybody in this clan ever questioned these unwritten rules.

Her presence in the woods hadn't been ignored by the adults. A group of elderly men stood on the other side of the playground and observed her watching their children playing; they didn't come to her or move away from their spot.

Lucy understood. She, too, would be concerned by the security of her children, if someone unknown stood still and watched them. These men seemed old, but, peering close, she realized they were in their fifties and sixties; this was the age group she wanted to talk to in her mission. She traversed the clearing through the rackets of the children and then went toward these men. They made desperate signs for her to go away, but, when Lucy kept up with her steps, they held their ground and examined her from head to feet.

Lucy reached these men and greeted them, but they didn't say a word; the whites of their watery eyes bulged in fear.

She asked if they had lived with this clan for the year she was interested in; they didn't open their mouths to reply. She realized they might not speak or know French well. She repeated her question slowly, and then rephrased it in English and Spanish. These men, still in the grip of their fear, fidgeted and glanced over their shoulders. Elderly women appeared at the doors of their hovels and beckoned their men over, but these men didn't move from where they were; they kept making signs for Lucy to leave these woods. Finally, one among these men took out a phone and called someone in a language she didn't understand.

Fifteen minutes later, a sleek black car, unlike the other beaten down vehicles of this clan, rolled into the woods and stopped before them. A stout man in his late forties or early fifties, his hair tousled and eyes red, emerged from the expensive car, slammed its door, and stood before her. Lucy noticed the recent scratches on his face, and then saw the blood marks dried around his collar and over the shoulder. The man claimed he was the chief of this clan and, if she had any concerns about his people or their affairs, she should talk to him.

Lucy asked the same question, and the chief's eyes flared.

"I was here," the man said. "My father was the chief then."

"Is he still here?"

"No."

"Where is he?"

"In heaven."

"I'm trying to help someone."

"Ask me then."

Lucy stated her inquiry concerned a murder at this periphery in that year. A man was convicted wrongly for this crime, and she was trying to find information to liberate him. If anyone in this clan had witnessed that murder then and would come forward now to testify in favor of this man, she would pay whatever financial compensation they demanded. The mention of murder had stiffened the chief, but the prospect of reward loosened his body and eased his face into a skewed smile.

"The convict is liberated already," the chief said.

"Pardon?"

"He was living in that camp with the African migrants."

"You know him?"

"You don't."

The chief declared he had seen this convicted felon rise from the pit of a French prison to the altar of an international hero. If she was trying to help this man by spying around his clan, she was wasting her time and his. If she had no other questions for him, she should leave him and his clan alone; he had other urgent matters in his hands to deal with.

Lucy thanked the chief for his time then left this group of men.

On her way out, the same elderly woman, with her bursting eyes, made illegible signs with her hands and uttered incomprehensible words from her foaming mouth, but then, one of the older men, with his eyes lowered, appeared at the side of this woman, wrapped his arm around her shoulders, and led her away from Lucy's path.

Lucy watched them go, and then went out of the woods.

The ambulance trailed the police car into the construction site. Arnault looked on both sides of their passage; he didn't see any accidents. The frenzied call to their squad hadn't clarified the emergency; as far as he could see, all the scaffoldings stood intact, and no crowd gathered anywhere on this site. The two vehicles rolled to the end of the passage then turned into the area that housed the migrant workers in the company's mobile homes and trailers.

The police car entered the alley of Zala's family and continued in the direction of their trailer. A throng of disturbed migrants milled about the open door of the trailer where Zala's mother stood on the stoop and wiped her eyes. Arnault stopped the vehicle behind the police car and jumped down with his emergency kit. A female police officer started talking to Zala's father. Arnault caught the snippets of their flurried exchange and guessed what he would see inside that trailer. He braced his rising fear, nodded at the distressed faces he knew here, then wedged through the crowd and reached Zala's mother at the door.

She descended from the staircase without looking at him.

Inside, the first aid agents of the construction company were going on with their cardiac massage. They saw Arnault and his colleagues; they shook their heads then moved away from Zala. The loosened rope was still wound around her neck. While his colleagues fitted their instruments on her, Arnault lifted her head, took the nylon rope off, and felt the wound from the fall that had occurred when the rope was cut in rush by her neighbors. He saw the chipped corner of the counter that had hit the back of her head during this fall.

Her heart started pumping again, but the signals from her brain became unstable. Arnault alternated the massage with the oxygen. Zala's eyes opened once, registered Arnault for a few seconds, then looked far and closed their lids. Two pearls of tears rolled down her cheeks then dropped onto the floor of linoleum. Arnault kept up with his procedures and went on talking to her, but the signals from her brain kept falling; her skin no longer flinched from the drops of sweat that dribbled from

Arnault's forehead onto her face.

Her chest heaved once then fell; her heart sent no more signals. Her face contorted once and then released. Her limbs convulsed a couple of times, then slowed to a twitch and stopped. The signals from her brain faded away, and the screens went blank. Arnault stopped his work, knelt at her side, and waited.

Zala didn't return. The soul of this violated African beauty had fled, but left behind her indelible charm.

Arnault made a cross over his chest. He rose to his feet, hugged Zala's two younger siblings in his arms, and then left their trailer. He was braving through the cries of his former friends and heading straight to his vehicle, when Zala's mother called him over and handed him a note. Arnault wiped his face and let his bleared eyes focus on the letters.

The words were written in haste, but they did come from Zala's hand. What those words stated clenched his jaws and stiffened the muscles of his legs and arms. The cold hand of Zala's mother touched his hot cheek. Arnault lowered his eyes; he saw what his impulses were asking him to do wasn't good.

He took the note to the policewoman and gave her the name of the cleaning company Zala worked for. The officer frowned at the note; she took out her phone and called her station. Arnault reached out to Zala's father, squeezed his shoulders, and then went toward his vehicle. A thought occurred to him along the way. He stopped and searched around for Isayas, but he didn't see the boy anywhere in the crowd. He asked his colleague to drive the vehicle to their squad; he would join them there after a short walk on the bank of the Seine.

16

The chief's words, coming as a bolt, had stunned Lucy in the woods, and then pushed her into the wrong conclusion. But now, as her feet moved on the bridge again, her blind spot emerged before her and made her stop. She had made an error of bias and this wasn't the way to go.

She rolled back in time.

Arnault was all over the news after rescuing that child. The media surrounded the camp at the periphery for a week and glorified his life with the migrants there. Then they ranted against his past in prison, raved about his days since release, rallied his meeting with the president, and revved up his roles with the rescue squad.

The chief of this clan must have seen all that. No doubt he seemed rougher than she had thought, but, in her haste to help Arnault, she had connected his clan too quickly to that murder at this periphery twenty-four years ago.

Need breeds mirage; what we seek in impatience rushes to us on illusions. She knew this truth because she had lived it several times before.

Her experience with this clan had biased her against them. And, by allowing her bias to confirm her suspicion, she had violated the basic principle of justice: the presumption of innocence. Arnault's deposition from twenty-four years ago did confirm the hand of vagrants in that murder, but his statements never tied this particular clan to that crime. In fact, his declaration clearly stated he didn't know where these attackers had come from. This clan's living near the site of the crime didn't confirm in any ways their involvement in it.

Besides, the site of this old factory had housed criminals for nearly half a century. The authorities might have evacuated this site several times over that period; she had no concrete information on any of this. There was no guarantee this same clan had occupied this site for all these years and, only by her personal prejudice against their chief, she had connected them to that murder.

A false suspicion had cost Arnault twenty-three years of his life behind the bars. In her impatience to exonerate him into innocence, she couldn't send another innocent person from this clan to prison through her biased suspicions. That would be the biggest of all ironies. She knew about the recent arrests from this clan. After meeting their chief today, she also knew his ways weren't necessarily always honest. But the eyes of the code separated the acts—this was the law—and she couldn't allow her impression of this chief to taint her judgment against his entire clan, particularly after seeing those signs of humanity among them.

Besides, Arnault, from his personal experience with the law, must be sensitive to this injustice of bias; he wouldn't appreciate any illegal presumptions of guilt arising from her unethical prejudices. As an amateur investigator, she was prone to the errors of her emotions, and those errors could ruin someone's life. If she wanted to go any farther along this route for Arnault, she would have to be more careful about not letting any forms of prejudice seep into her head and cloud her vision.

She leaned her hip against the railing and looked over the Seine. The winding river, with its nonstop traffic, disappeared at the bend then reappeared in the suburbs. From this point on the high bridge, she could see the river zigzag through neighboring towns, and then stretch beyond like a chopped cord of silver through the waning rays of the sun; silhouettes of tall trees, vaunting autumn colors, alternated with deep dark bushes and broke the river's twisted strand.

She placed those towns in her head, but she couldn't remember their names; except for the one her father used to take her to for her rowing lessons. She recalled the notorious eddies in the Seine from those days and, looking below, she saw she was standing directly above one of those whirlpools. Bubbles rose from its depth into the rolling folds of wakes that came from the passing barges. They spoke of the undertow that roiled the water and mud under the surface of the Seine.

She moved away from the railing then continued over the bridge. The work at the construction site had stopped for the day. From this height, she could see the tramline skirt the periphery of the city. The police car and the ambulance she had seen earlier now rolled toward the circular road without their sirens and strobes. A man in firefighter's uniform emerged from the tunnel then hurried on the sidewalk under the overpass toward this bridge.

Her feet stopped again.

It wasn't so much the words of the chief that bothered her this time; it was the way he had uttered those words and the way his body movements had added nuances to those words that bothered her. She closed her eyelids and replayed their meeting.

She saw the glare in the chief's eyes at the mention of the year. She saw his body stiffen and his face glower at the mention of the murder. And she saw the flickers in his irises at the mention of her financial reward. She saw his disheveled hair, the fresh scratches over his face, and the dried bloodstains around his collar and on his shoulders. She had gone there to investigate a murder and she saw now what had affected her perception of this clan; she couldn't be the only person to suspect them of wrongdoings on the margin of society.

The source of her error of bias lay right there.

She placed herself in the chief's position. She saw she, too, would have his language on her body and his expressions on her face. Besides, the chief knew his clan was occupying a place not designated for their living. A harsh life leaves its marks on you, but not necessarily of crime. The prejudices that had shown her earlier the nonexistent links were now tainting her perceptions with nuances of guilt. She wasn't fit to investigate this matter any further. She shivered at the thought of someone spying on her the way she had done with this clan.

She saw the error in her offer of financial reward too. Even if someone from this clan had witnessed the murder twenty-four years ago, the chief couldn't ask the person to come forward and testify for money; the law would pin both for impeding justice, and the chief seemed smart enough to know that. Besides, after all these years, their testimony would serve nothing in locating the murderer unless the perpetrator was someone they personally knew. She had been impulsive in her act; she should have thought about all this before coming here; but, so far, her actions had harmed no one and wouldn't harm anyone if she stopped now. She turned back to look at the hovels of this clan one last time before leaving them behind her.

She saw the three men on the far end of the bridge.

She recognized the chief, but not the other two members of his clan; they were younger than the ones she had seen in the woods. Their steps came fast, but they didn't move in a rush. The chief might have changed his mind about her offer for reward. Her reflex had sent her hands to grip the straps of her purse, but, seeing their measured gaits and their calm movements, she released her grip and then stood there facing them.

They weren't menacing her; she, too, wanted to put them at ease.

Arnault knew rapes were common in domestic works. But, he also knew they happened to women who worked for cash and didn't dare to report. In her days of working for cash, Zala used to employ her instincts to filter people, but, in her new job with this cleaning company, she had no choice over her clients. The company had asked for her criminal records before sending her to people's homes, but Arnault doubted they ever checked anything on their clients; too many cleaning company in Paris pitched for these same clients.

He crossed the ethnic marketplace along the tramline, open at this hour as usual and teeming with people he knew; he didn't stop this time to chat with them. In his new outfits, none of them recognized him either. He took the tunnel that had once been his home, avoided looking at the place where Zala's family had lived, and continued on the sidewalk under the overpass toward the woods.

He trusted the commissariat would do their diligence with the cleaning company and Zala's note to nail her rapist. But something else lay in the shadows of her words that made him suspect the act had been planned and the place set up for this purpose; he needed to check his hunch with care, in order to avoid drawing in an innocent by wrong suspicions.

He rolled his memory back to his days with the migrants' camp here.

He saw, camouflaged among the multitude of relief workers, the aged perverts on prowl during their promenades of nonchalance. He saw them picking their favorites from the camp, pointing those out to the pimps, and then haggling over their objects of desire. He saw the face of that ancient bourgeois he had taken by the collar and thrown out of the tunnel under the glaring eyes of those pimps.

Isayas knew the cleaning company Zala worked for. The boy wouldn't descend so far as to sell his sister, but he might have mentioned the name of her company to this chief of vagrants he worked for now. Given the amount of time he spent with this clan, he could have slipped out the name during a casual conversation with any of its members, without thinking about the consequences of his act. Before drawing any premature conclusions on the involvement of this clan in Zala's rape, it was important to speak to Isayas. The state of their parents had stopped Arnault from asking them about their boy; he wondered if Isayas knew what had happened to his sister and for how long he hadn't returned to see his family.

The road reached the border of the Seine then continued along its bend. He saw the hovels in the woods on the far bank and the smokes that rose from their chimneys. He doubted the chief and his assistants or Isayas would be there at this time, but it was worth trying. The sun had sunk behind the crest of the circular road, but its rays from below lit the railings of the high bridge that crossed the Seine at this point; he saw the silhouette of a lone woman leaning against those railings on the bridge.

Arnault left the sidewalk then climbed the staircase to the bridge.

He saw the lone woman at the midpoint of the bridge. She had her back turned toward him, but he recalled seeing her earlier on the sidewalk before the tunnel while driving to the construction site with his colleagues. Now she watched three men coming toward her from the far end and there was no one else on this bridge.

Arnault knew the three approaching men.

He recognized the woman too.

And the way she stood facing them showed she knew these three men and she wasn't afraid of them. He had no clues to what this lawyer woman from the commissariat was up to here at this hour, but she had failed to see the intention of this chief and his two assistants behind their measured steps and composed gaits.

They were coming at her.

Contrary to Lucy's expectation, the chief and his two companions didn't slow before her.

A male voice called out and warned her from the back. Lucy glanced over her shoulder and saw the man in firefighter's uniform running toward them from the other end of the bridge. The chief kept coming straight at her, but the two younger men separated from him, went aside, and surrounded her against the railing.

Lucy swung her purse, whacked the young man to her right on the face, kicked the youth behind her in the groin, then dropped her handbag and punched the chief on the face. The chief stopped, rubbed his nose, and spat on her. The two younger men came over their surprise, regained their balance, then stared at the chief and waited for his orders.

Footsteps scurried behind her, but Lucy kept her gaze fixed on these three men.

The chief eyed his assistants and stepped forward. Lucy cocked her elbow and lifted her fist. The chief deflected her blow then caught her head by the hair. The two assistants grabbed her at the waist and the thighs, tried to lift her off, but she tore their faces with her nails and plunged her knees into their abdomens. The two assistants fell back again, but the chief ignored her punishing hands and feet, and dragged her by the hair toward the railing.

The running footsteps sounded nearer.

The chief pulled her head down then banged her face on the railing. She collapsed to the pavement. He grabbed her at the torso, tried to lift her and throw her off the bridge, but she caught the bars of the railing, folded her legs, and thrust him with her full force in the chest; she couldn't release the chief's grip on her or budge him by an inch. The two assistants kicked her in the ribs and strived to grab her thrashing legs.

She heard the thwacks and the clacks.

The two assistants grunted and groaned, and the chief's hands went off her head. Whacks and cracks came in a row. The two assistants thumped to the pavement, and the chief went neck-to-neck with the man in firefighter's clothes.

Lucy rose from the pavement and recognized Arnault.

Blood squirted down from her nostrils and fell on her blouse. More blood streamed around her brows, blurred her eyes, and dribbled down her cheeks. Her head reeled and her ears fizzed, but she grabbed the upper rail and steadied her feet. The two assistants covered their smashed faces, whimpered, and rolled about the pavement.

Arnault heaved and came free. He stepped back and threw a punch at the chief's temple, but the chief ducked the blow, leaped forward, and clutched Arnault's windpipe. Arnault choked. His both fists worked like a machine on the chief's torso, but the man didn't let his grip on Arnault's windpipe go.

Lucy took her shoe off and beat the chief's head. Arnault caught the chief's wrist and tried to wrench his hand off. The chief still didn't release his grip on Arnault's throat.

Lucy cracked the sole of her shoe on the chief's head. Arnault threshed the chief at the chest and at the shoulders; he thrashed around and writhed from side to side, but he still couldn't free his windpipe from the chief's grip; his desperate efforts only sapped his energy and burnt his stock of oxygen.

Arnault's eyes bulged and his face turned blue. The chief growled and stated he had spared Arnault's life twenty-four years ago, but now Arnault would die here in his hands, along with this slimy whore who had gone snooping on his clan.

The cold confession pumped Lucy's adrenaline to the peak.

She threw the broken shoe, took a deep breath, then gathered all her strengths and kicked the chief at the back of his knee. The chief's leg buckled. His hand came off Arnault's windpipe, but then he regained his balance and charged at Arnault. The two men locked together again, then tilted over the railings and raged at a new battle.

Once more, the chief's hand found its way to Arnault's throat. Lucy kept kicking at the back of the chief's knees, but, with the man's weight supported by the upper rails now, her kicks did nothing to tip his balance.

The two men toppled over the railing. They tumbled in their death grip and splashed into the Seine. The water rose in fury, then closed around them and covered their bodies. Lucy bent over the railing and peered into the river; only bubbles rose from its depth and broke in the folds at the surface. Then the wakes from a passing barge drowned those bubbles too.

Lucy dug her phone out of the purse then called for help.

The scuffle continued under water, but not for long.

Arnault's trainings in underwater rescue and his capacity of apnea larger than others gave him the edge over the strife. The grip on his windpipe released, and a downward current pulled the chief's limp body into the mud. Arnault tried to pull the man out of the current, but a whirlpool caught the chief and took his body out of Arnault's reach.

Arnault's breath was running out. He swam up to the surface, filled his lungs, then took off his shoes and removed his uniform. The strong current took these items fast out of his view. A barge was coming his way from upstream. He swam in the direction of the current and found a rapids that pulled him out of the barge's reach. The wakes came charging at him, went over his head, then clashed against the shore and broke into foams.

Arnault kept out of the two lanes for the barges. He turned over on his back and let the fast current carry him along the river's shore.

The banks on both sides hid in the dark. Arnault thought the rapids might have carried him a few hundred meters at the most, but he couldn't recognize these suburbs on the river. The steep walls rising from the river told him he was crossing an area of docklands. He didn't see any stairs or ladders rising from the water. In his state of exhaustion, he didn't dare to climb up any of the pillars that rose from the river to these piers. The Seine slowed and then accelerated again. He kept his body afloat and his chin above the water; he rode the wakes from the passing barges; and he let the current carry him along its course.

Twice more, he found himself caught in whirlpools, but his trainings pulled him out both times. He saw he was crossing one of the wealthy suburbs of Paris. Houses of significant sizes appeared along both banks, separated by tall hedges and thick bushes. Among the trees, the streetlights glowed over the water and showed no bubbling patches on the surface that signaled underwater turmoil. Arnault rolled over and swam toward the shore.

But the Seine narrowed again into rapids.

The strong current carried him out of the hamlets into farmlands. He missed the pile of a bridge and ended into another whirlpool stronger than before. He swam out again and felt he was reaching the end of his limits. He gave up swimming; he returned to staying afloat on his back; and he saved his energy for the next whirlpool.

No more houses came on either side of the Seine; only reeds and bushes lined both shores. No more whirlpools caught him either; only barges kept going in both lanes and rocking him with their wakes. He remained on his back and paddled with his hands toward the shore. The waves from the passing boats helped him in his moves.

His feet hit an obstacle and his head turned with the current. Arnault straightened himself in the water and caught the gnarled roots of the weeping willow. He reached up, grabbed a drooping branch, then dragged himself out of the water and paused to breathe.

The bank here came steep. He tried to stand, but his head turned, and he almost fell in the water. He crawled on four up the bank, couldn't gather his strength to climb over the parapet that lined the top, then found a ledge at its bottom and lay down on his back.

Water gurgled among the roots tangled below. Arnault tried a couple of times to rise, but his limbs refused to move. He tried to figure the time from the position of the moon, but he couldn't lift his head or raise his torso. He strained his ears and tried to listen, but he only heard the water lapping and gurgling along the shore.

The sounds lulled him.

He drifted to a slumber then descended into a deep sleep.

17

The ambulance came for Lucy. She refused to go with them. She waited for the rescuers to begin their search for Arnault in the Seine before giving her deposition to the policewoman who had come with the rescue squad. Then she stayed on the bridge ignoring the ache that hammered inside her head and the pressure that built up behind her eyes; the rescue squad couldn't get her to climb into their ambulance.

At the end, her father arrived and convinced her that she wasn't adding any value to the search by staying at the scene; she would do better going to the hospital and returning to shape for Arnault. The officer thanked her father then signed her off to the hospital; the two younger assailants had already been hauled off to the police station.

At the hospital, Lucy ignored the doctors and followed the rescue live on the television.

A special force from the marine joined the rescue squad. The divers combed through the bed of the Seine, both upstream and downstream, from the source of the river to its mouth. They recovered the bloated corpse of the vagrant chief stuck in the mud, but they didn't find any trace of Arnault anywhere. The newscaster announced this national hero had saved the same woman from the hands of vagrants for the second time and then vanished into the turgid water of the Seine.

The policewoman came to the hospital with their technicians, lifted the strains of DNA left on Lucy by her three attackers, and sent those to their judicial laboratory for testing; Lucy didn't take her eyes off the television and her phone for a second. Finally, her mother dozed away at her side; her father went out, brought back a newspaper and a coffee, and kept up his vigilance on her. Lucy didn't notice any of the activities of her parents.

The camera zoomed onto the scene of crime. Lucy saw the point on the high bridge from where Arnault had fallen into the Seine, and then she heard the details of her attack she had given to the policewoman; the newscaster <u>confirmed no knives</u> had been found on any of her three assailants. A former picture of Lucy appeared next to the condemned law firm she used to work for before, and then the camera moved to the grills of the tribunal of Paris where her office of the public defenders was now. The newscaster added it remained unclear to them at this point what this single female lawyer in her thirties, from an elite family of lawyers in Versailles, had been doing over that deserted bridge on the periphery of Paris at that hour.

Lucy's father lifted his eyes from the paper and then raised his eyebrows.

The camera went back in time to Arnault's intervention at the construction site before her attack. He was called there for the death of a woman he had lived with in the migrants' camp at the periphery. The photo of a young African woman appeared on the screen. This woman Zala had committed suicide after being raped at a job for the cleaning company she worked for. Her brother, Isayas, disappeared after her rape; the boy had a record of arrest in Paris for theft; her parents suspected he might be out there looking for his sister's rapist to settle account. The photo of the boy was placed on the screen next to his dead sister's.

Lucy recognized this Isayas; she had defended him one night at the tribunal of Paris. She remembered the boy's association with the vagrants and recalled the reprimand the judge had given him in front of her before his release.

The newscaster moved on with the story.

After his intervention at the construction site, Arnault didn't return to his squad. His colleagues saw him depressed from the death of this woman Zala he loved and from his failure to bring her back to life. He told his colleagues he was going for a walk by the Seine. His former acquaintances from the quarter then saw him walking through the market, sad and silent, and heading toward the tunnel where he had lived with Zala. He reached the bank of the Seine where he used to stroll with Zala and then met his misfortune on the bridge by saving Lucy from the vagrants.

Lucy flushed. She sat up against the headboard and rubbed her face. The sharp stings reminded her of the splint over her broken nose and of the stitches in the raw skin over her lacerated forehead.

The newscaster held up a portrait of Zala and Arnault together.

According to this family of African migrants, Zala cared for Arnault when he reached their camp with the injuries he received from saving Lucy the first time from vagrants. He fell in love with Zala; she was a woman of exquisite beauty and immaculate character. Their love deepened through his living with her for three months in that tunnel. Then rescuing that child lifted Arnault out of their camp, placed him in the rescue squad, and separated him from Zala. Afterward, his colleagues never saw him with another woman.

These two unfortunate lovers—after coming from two separate margins of the society, after meeting at this camp at the periphery then making this tunnel their home for a few short months, after being forced to go their separate ways—had met at death probably.

"They're exaggerating about the two!" Lucy turned off the television. "They're raising this other woman to heaven and lowering Arnault to grave already!" She pulled out the tubes plugged on her. "Someone should tell them to keep their theories to themselves!"

Her mother sprang up from her slumber. Her father closed the newspaper, rose without a word from the chair, and went out of the room. He returned with the nurse, but Lucy didn't want those tubes back on her again. She was surprised by her own reactions. She glanced at her parents; their faces registered no surprises or shocks. She thanked the nurse for coming over, and then went back to watching the television and the screen of her phone.

No fresh news about Arnault from anywhere yet.

The first rays of the dawn streamed in through the panes of the window and streaked her face. She took a few sips of the fluid next to her, then lay down and tried to keep her head busy by planning the steps of Arnault's new trial.

The planning helped. The steps of Arnault's trial felt more real than the unreal she was seeing and hearing about him in the media. Yet she couldn't deny the reality unfolding around him before her eyes by the hours. The trial she had been planning for so meticulously over these past months would never see the courtroom unless Arnault returned alive. Death had extinguished all pursuits against this vagrant chief, but she didn't want Arnault to go with the stigma of someone else's crime on his back. Before dying, the chief had confessed to that crime; what used to be a remote possibility before now stood out with glaring certainty.

Her telephone beeped. A message from the officer informed she had news; Lucy grabbed her phone and called the station.

"The lab results came this morning," the officer said.

"And?"

"The strains lifted from you have matched the three assailants."

"Uh-huh."

"No surprise there," the officer said. "But the DNA lifted from the chief has also matched a strain in Arnault's dossier from twenty-four years ago."

No surprise there either. Lucy thanked her then asked if there was any further news about Arnault. The policewoman stated she had received some tentative information on this front, but she was waiting for further confirmation, and she couldn't confide those new developments to Lucy over the phone. Lucy declared she was coming to the commissariat right now and then hung up the call.

Her parents followed her out of the room. Her mother complained what she was doing wasn't reasonable by any means. Lucy told her mother that every act in this world couldn't be explained by reasons. Her father stayed by her side and didn't utter a word.

The doctor put up a stiff resistance. The results of her brain scan didn't look good. The edema could return at any moment and threaten her life. Her mother agreed and murmured up a protest. Lucy reminded them that the rescuer missing in the Seine faced a higher threat to his life. She pulled those tubes off an hour ago, and nothing had happened to her since.

The doctor didn't want to sign her release.

Lucy asserted she knew her rights. She confirmed she was in a sound state of mind; she was able to carry out all her functions in full autonomy; and she was leaving the hospital on her own responsibility. She thanked the doctor and his team for their services. She signed the papers for her voluntary release. She assured them their care had restored her to health and she would return to them if she needed their services again.

The doctor understood. He signed his part of the release, gave her precautions to follow, and then let her go.

Outside, Lucy thanked her parents for their support. She excused herself for the inconveniences caused to them by her circumstances. She assured them they could return to their home now and remain confident that she would be safe on her own hereafter.

Her parents refused to go.

Lucy insisted, but her parents stood there looking at the ground. She saw no resentments or reproaches on them; she saw worry and sorrow. She put herself in their places, felt what they felt, then took the key of her apartment out and gave it to them. She started going toward the station for taxis, but her father led her by the shoulder toward their car. Her mother collected their overnight bag from the trunk then took the stairs down to the metro.

Inside the car, her father took the address of the commissariat from her. He started the engine, placed his palm on her forearm, then nodded once and pulled away from the curb. Lucy understood. She tried to keep her mind off the new developments she was about to discover at the commissariat. She wasn't sure the officer would reveal those to her.

Lucy saw her error on the way to the commissariat.

The officer hadn't clarified the match. She had no reasons to, because it concerned Arnault alone; she might not remember Lucy was in charge of his former case through the association. Legally, the officer couldn't divulge anything about this case until Lucy provided her the proofs, and she didn't have anything on her to prove. The car reached the periphery of Paris by the Seine, then turned along the bend of the river and headed toward the tunnel. A row of bulldozers rumbled and rolled in the direction of the woods.

At the moment of the chief's confession, by impulse, she had connected this man to the fugitive murderer from twenty-four years ago. Three criminals had left their DNAs on Arnault, but only one of those three had matched the strain recovered from the slain woman's clothes, liberated Arnault, and kept him on the hook for a potential accomplice. This chief could also be one of those two other criminals from before who had acted in concert with the woman's murderer and spared Arnault's life, for him to take the blame of that crime.

A new trial required the identification of the murderer.

Unless the match from this morning tied the vagrant chief to the strain left on the dead woman, he couldn't legally be pinned down as her murderer; he would only be identified as one of the other two criminals present on the scene of that crime twenty-four years ago.

But the situation wasn't entirely hopeless.

At the time of that crime, this chief's father was the chief of that clan. If the father had slain that woman, and the son had acted as his assistant, the father's DNA left on her would still match his son's via offspring link and could be used in a new trial to exonerate Arnault. No juror, in a sane state of mind, after seeing and hearing what Arnault had done since his release, would see him as a potential accomplice to that crime from twenty-four years ago.

To get to a new trial for the old case, she needed a significant new element, and the fresh DNA match from this morning had given her that element.

Her mind was working clearly again.

The fresh match would also fit Arnault's deposition from twenty-four years ago. By the time he reached the site of that crime, the woman's throat had already been slit; the two other men had appeared from somewhere in the dark during his scuffle with her killer. Besides, last evening, Arnault might have recognized the chief during their strife over the bridge; he would be there at this new trial to clarify that point before the jury.

A dull pressure wrung her chest. She checked her phone for further information about Arnault, didn't find anything more on the news sites and the social media networks than she knew already, and turned on the car's radio. They no longer talked about him. The new developments in the search for Arnault were being held back from the media and the public for some reason. She forced the fears into a corner of her mind and took in the crowded market the car navigated through.

She glanced at her father at the wheel. His face showed no irritation, anxiety, or fatigue. He returned her glance by batting an eye; she saw in that wink far more than a silent approval. A new side of her father was emerging that she had never seen before. She knew her father was keeping tabs on Arnault too and she wondered if he was holding back something from her that he had come to know. She saw they had reached the commissariat. She told her father to park the car, and then she went through the security of the station.

The policewoman received Lucy then led her to an interview room.

She stated the two attackers in detention had confessed about their plan to throw Lucy off the bridge. The prosecutor had already opened a case against them at the tribunal, but they would stay at the commissariat for now due to the new elements revealing about their clan.

She informed that the association had called this morning and asked for the results of the new DNA tests. She knew Lucy was the lawyer designated for Arnault's dossier, but, given her current state of health, she had faxed a copy of the results to the association, and another copy to the office of the head prosecutor at the tribunal of Paris; as far as she could see on their system, a new case had already been opened since then. She gave Lucy the case number and a copy of the DNA test results from this morning.

Lucy saw the match was direct and not through offspring link.

The officer confided that the fresh developments in the search for Arnault were still nascent and she asked Lucy to keep this information confidential: Arnault's uniform was recovered last night from the rudder of a barge. A team had searched the hulls and the bottoms of all the barges that had crossed the Seine since his disappearance. One of his shoes was found stuck in a bush at the break of dawn about sixty kilometers from where he had fallen, and the other of the pair was found six hours later at the mouth of the Seine. A team of divers had ransacked the floor of the English Channel near the estuary and recovered both of his socks. One shoe might have come off during the struggle, but the recovery of all these other items showed he had survived the battle then taken those off to swim. A third team with sniff dogs was going from door to door along the course of the river and enquiring citizens for the slightest signs of Arnault.

The president of the Republique had asked them to spare no means in this search.

The officer agreed, given the number of hours passed, hopes were waning for others, but she wasn't giving up on Arnault yet. She had met him at the construction site during his intervention on that migrant African woman Zala; she believed no news about Arnault only meant good news about him.

Lucy thanked the officer and asked her about Zala.

The officer stated the suicide had occurred in her jurisdiction, but not the rape. She didn't have the exact details of the pursuits for the rapist, but the investigators from the commissariat of Le Marais had come close to nailing someone for that rape. The disappearance of Zala's brother, Isayas, fell under her jurisdiction, and she knew Lucy had represented this boy before an instructing judge at the tribunal of Paris for theft. Since his disappearance, a number of street cameras had caught this boy going toward the clan of vagrants in the woods. This fitted his scheme of revenge the media claimed, but, since then, her investigators had dug up other elements about this clan to believe the contrary; she had signed off the order to dismantle this clan from the woods.

Lucy told her what she had seen inside this clan.

The officer noted the details then confirmed the chief's exploitations of his people. The death of this chief and the arrest of his assistants would liberate those individuals captive to this clan: the handicapped they kept as prisoners for begging; the harem of women they kept to prostitute and produce children; the old and the ill they kept for forced labor. She confessed, in her entire career, she had never come across such a vicious clan and, without Lucy's intervention, all these exploitations could have continued for years before the authorities came to know; Lucy should have no regrets for this.

Lucy enquired what the authorities planned to do with the clan's children.

The officer stated the children belonged to the adults. Legally, she could do nothing for these children unless their parents gave them up. The clan members were free to take their children with them. Social aids were available in such cases and her report would entitle them for these aids, but nobody could force anything on them legally. She could only make sure the social workers reached out to them with aids from the government, but the clan members had all the rights to refuse those aids.

Lucy asked if Zala's family had a lawyer for her case.

The officer understood. She admitted she didn't know, but, if Lucy wanted a lawyer from her office of public defenders to represent Zala's family, she would like to know; she could send the case numbers for Zala to Lucy's office at the tribunal of Paris. Lucy noted down the two case numbers and then took the forms she needed to represent Zala's family.

Zala's parents signed the papers for their daughter. Lucy avoided looking at the young woman's photo on their table; it evoked more than anger and grief; it provoked feelings inappropriate for this moment and put her conscience at the feet of shame.

She decided to be frank with Zala's parents.

She told them she knew about Arnault and their daughter. She wasn't doing this only for Zala; she was doing this also for Arnault. She had no idea where Arnault was at this moment, but she was doing what Arnault would have liked to see done for Zala.

She vowed she couldn't bring their daughter back from heaven, but she would make sure the French justice descended Zala's violator to the rock bottom of hell and rubbed his face against the embers glowing there.

Then she ran out of their trailer.

She stormed into the car, covered her face, and broke into a sob. The hot tears pouring out of her didn't well up for Arnault or Zala; they took their source from a fear she had denied until now, and she could no longer hide it after seeing those signs in their trailer.

The media had not made up the stories about their love.

Her father's hand touched the back of her head. She lifted her face and saw the migrants gathered around their car. Her father handed her a tissue. She wiped her face then told him to head for the tribunal of Paris. The tears had cleaned her mind and released the pressure behind her eyes; she saw clearer now.

Their car rolled down the alley. In the rearview mirror, she noticed

Zala's parents standing at the door of their trailer and watching the car pull away.

They reached the tribunal of Paris.

The instructing judge frowned at the tapes and bandages on Lucy. He took the papers for Zala's case, but then confirmed that, to represent Arnault in his new trial, she needed to obtain his signature first. Lucy told him she was already in charge of Arnault's dossier through the association, but, as soon as she saw Arnault in person, she would have him sign the papers necessary for his representation.

The judge asked her to constitute a civil party in the case of her own assault by the vagrants. Lucy told him she would leave the case in the hands of the state, but, on the day of their trial, she would help the prosecutor with her testimonies against them.

On her way out of the judge's cabinet, Lucy ran into a court clerk and scattered the legal documents on the floor. Her father crouched, gathered the files, and handed those back to the clerk. Twice she avoided obstacles that didn't exist on her way, and once more she banged against a bailiff who stood right in front of her eyes.

Finally, her father led her by the shoulder toward the exit.

Lucy lay on the couch and kept her eyes on the television.

The camera zoomed on the dismantled camp of the clan of vagrants then moved to a mound of earth at the edge of the woods. The body of young Isayas, maimed and mutilated, had been dug out of that pit, along with the instruments used for the kill. The two younger assailants of Lucy, still detained at the commissariat, had confessed to the killing of this boy under the command of their chief.

The newscaster elaborated the circumstances of this brutal murder.

Isayas had given this chief the name of his sister's cleaning company for the promise of money. After her rape, the chief claimed the old pervert hadn't paid them for connecting him to Zala's company. Isayas saw through this lie and attacked the chief in fury. They killed him in the woods then shoved his body under the dirt with their knives. The DNA strains recovered on the boy and the knives had matched the three attackers of Lucy.

The camera shifted to the posh quarters of Le Marais.

The old pervert, a merchant banker retired from the French bank under fire, had called the cleaning company under a false name and insisted on Zala being sent to a place he had rented under the same name; the credit card transactions had revealed his identity through a labyrinth of circuits. Already on the radar of the authorities for suspected cruelty on migrant women, they had failed until now to tie him to a particular abuse, lacking concrete proofs and testimonies from women. A family man in his eighties, with three children to his score and five more for grandchildren, he had always used false names and a credit card issued under the identities of his mistress to rent his love nests.

The newscaster held up the photo of a decent woman in her thirties.

When this young mistress was hauled into the commissariat and charged with complicity in the crime against Zala, she fainted from the shock. Upon recovering, she broke in tears, denied all involvements, and claimed the credit card was on her name, but her lover had full control over its use, and the bills were paid directly from his account; the trails of the card's transactions and the statements obtained from her bank had confirmed these truths.

The camera zoomed on the façade of a townhouse covered with

thick growths of ivy.

The investigators linked the transactions for this particular love nest to the IP address of a public library in Le Marais. They discovered the old fool had used his real account there to make this reservation under a virtual name. The newscaster confirmed the patriarch's DNA had matched the strain found in Zala and on the linen left behind at this rented place.

Lucy's mouth tasted bitter.

She reached for the cup of water and drank a few more sips. She didn't feel like touching the food left by her mother on the low table in front of the sofa. High thirst and low appetite were the signs of fever; the rising headache confirmed she was running one.

The television channels had stopped talking about Arnault. Lucy picked up her phone; the news sites and the social media networks still waited for fresh news beyond what she already knew about him. She agreed with the officer from this morning at the commissariat: A man like Arnault couldn't just vanish under water; unless his body found its way into one of those former sewage canals that now drained rainwater from the gutters of Paris into the Seine; but, as far as she knew, all those sewage canals had grills on them.

Her amateur investigation had provoked this accident for Arnault, but it had also brought up on her the DNA match he needed for innocence. She held on to this twitching line of solace and hope that kept her from sinking into the silent mud of regrets and sorrow.

Her shifting eyes stopped on Arnault's stuff from Isle of Swans. They stood neater than she had left them before. She lifted her eyes and peeked at her parents sitting at the table. They looked tired, but they didn't seem ready to give up on her and go back to their big home of comfort; like her, they, too, had stayed in this small apartment to be closer to

Arnault.

"Does Arnault have a family?" her mother asked.

"I don't know."

"Have you checked?"

"No."

"Has anyone come forward?"

"Never."

For the first time Lucy realized she had never asked herself this question about Arnault. Whereas her parents were at her side now with their love and warmth, Arnault would have only the cold cares of the hospital when he returned from his mission; she couldn't see those cares substitute what she was receiving from her parents.

Lucy sat up on the sofa.

Her parents watched her, but not with an air of regret or reproach. Her father crossed his fingers on the table. Her mother parted her lips with a glint in the eyes, and then started talking. She regretted she could do little to reduce Lucy's anxiety for Arnault, but what she had to say might lessen her burden of guilt. If Lucy thought her act had inconvenienced her parents, she was wrong; it had rather produced effects to the contrary by opening their eyes.

Her mother glanced at her father and then went on speaking. People like them who lived on retirement annuities— who were upset by the fast and threatened by the abrupt; who ate three meals at fixed times, slept eight hours a day, and had their blood pressure and sugar level checked at regular intervals—were law abiding citizens who did only the required minimum when they saw someone in danger. They never got in troubles because they stayed away from troubles. Their difficulties to understand Lucy had come from seeing her actions from their perspectives, but those confusions lay in the past now. The events over the last twenty-four hours had changed their lenses; they now saw these same actions of hers through different eyes.

Lucy's vision blurred. She observed her mother's mouth opening and closing.

For example, her mother continued, Lucy could have easily forgotten Arnault after the first attack on her. Arnault had defended her from the vagrants; she had defended Arnault from the law. The account was settled. And, after Arnault rose through the rungs of glory by rescuing that child from the balcony, Lucy could have forgotten about his former conviction too; her actions were no longer vital for Arnault's survival. Acts like those didn't emerge solely from Lucy's feelings for him; they also rose from her conscience about the principle of fairness in justice. An innocent man, convicted from helping others, must not carry the brand of guilt on his back for life; he must be compensated for his compassion.

Lucy's face tingled. She watched her mother's jaws stiffen.

Her mother stated that people like Arnault at the periphery of life were exceptions to the normal. But this monstrous hero, this glorious convict, this savage civility with his contagious compassion, also set the norms for the detached normal like her.

She vowed she would never ask Lucy again what she was doing on the couch of that commissariat when she could return home and sleep in her bed. She promised she would never say again that the cell of a jail was better for a homeless man than the floor of his tent. She admitted she was too ashamed to ask Lucy's pardon for all these errors, but she would make sure to ask Arnault. She knew at her depth that, to pardon her for these prejudices against him, Arnault would return from where he was. And she could utter these words with certainty because she knew this condemned angel was generous beyond all limits.

Lucy's head reeled. She saw her mother's lips tremble.

Her mother went on speaking, but Lucy no longer listened; she had heard the knock on her door. She rose from the sofa, but then fell back. She told her parents she knew that knock. Arnault had come to sign his papers for her. They should open the door and let him in before he left thinking it was the wrong door.

Her mother stopped. Her father took out his phone and started talking.

Lucy tried to rise again. Her mother rushed over and stopped her from rolling onto the floor. Lucy pointed at her purse on the shelf. The papers with Arnault's details were in its inside pocket; she asked her mother to get those forms for him. Her mother held her tighter and told her not to worry; Arnault would be with her at any moment.

Her father stopped talking on the phone. He opened the door and let Arnault in. Other rescuers entered after Arnault. They took her from her mother. They lifted her, carried her down the stairs, and out of the building. They opened their van and laid her next to Arnault.

The vehicle pulled away and they moved on with her.

18

He dreamed of his childhood with parents and grandparents.

He saw his dog fall into the whirlpool then die before his eyes; he could do nothing to rescue the animal. Crickets creaked, grasshoppers rasped; cicadas seesawed, frogs croaked; a cat mewed, another shut it up.

He recalled his visits to the Science Museum with Maude. He thought of the female guard in prison and of the kind warden. They went when the orange beams rolled over his face, lit the infinite behind his eyelids in yellow, and bathed his face in soft warmth.

Hums and splashes came from the river. The wind picked up then fell again. A rodent's teeth crunched and ground. The source of light rose higher and its rays hit his face stronger. Flies buzzed, bees droned; crows cawed, jays cackled; ducks quacked, geese honked, and a lone eagle shrilled. Dull bills nibbled his toes. His eyes parted their lids, caught the glimpse of an adolescent swan, and then closed again.

He dreamed of his tent on Isle of Swans. He cooked under that bridge and swam in the Seine. He saw that awkward swan chick and it made him chuckle. He heard its parents trumpet and the seagulls laugh.

He remembered that female lawyer from the commissariat. Her firm defense before the officer didn't fit with her fumbling for words after his release. He tried to recall her name and see her face again, but the source of light disappeared behind his head and hid her features. The swishes, the squeaks, and the buzzes died away; the groans, the moans, and the drones remained.

An owl hooted then a fox howled. Ants climbed into his ears; a spider crawled over his face; and a lizard slithered across his torso. Nightingales crooned. A white glow appeared, cooled his face, and soothed his eyes.

He dreamed of his days with the migrants under the overpass. He saw Zala's family and his days with her in that tunnel. He heard the cries of that child hanging from the balcony. He shivered at that moment when after a near slip off, he paused for a breath, and the child, looking down at him from four floors above, almost let himself go; he had never climbed a wall that high. He wished the child's mother got the job she had interviewed for.

He saw his days with the rescue squad. Once more, he lived his failure to revive Zala and saw her fading away before his eyes. Once more his impulses for her violator returned; and, once more, he calmed his impulsions by recalling her firm words and warm cares.

He saw the lawyer from the commissariat on that bridge. Her name came to him this time. Her courage, her strength, and her tolerance of pain didn't match her looks, but fit her character nevertheless; they stirred feelings in him he didn't want to fathom. He tried to see her facial features, but his eyes failed. It wasn't the blood that covered her face; it was a veil of mistrust that rose between them and kept their distance.

Roosters crowed. The orange glow lit his eyes and warmed his face again. A horse neighed and a donkey brayed. Rowers went by talking on radios and splashing their oars. He heard the barking of a dog followed by a number of voices speaking. The wind rose, and then a fresh breeze swept over his nose. Odors of pines and resins flared his nostrils. Scents of wild berries and ripe fruits stirred his tongue and watered his mouth.

The dog barked nearer. Voices spoke above him.

He heard the sirens and the sounds of vehicles. He heard the commands of his trade, but he didn't recognize the voices they came from. The dog barked louder. Eight hands lifted him, placed him in a stretcher, and transferred him into an ambulance.

The dog bayed. The radios echoed his name and the commands he knew. The vehicle blew its siren, then rolled off and blasted away.

He could no longer hear the dog.

19

This wasn't a trial court she knew. The jurors here dressed in robes of judges. The trial took place on a podium in the open, surrounded by citizens from another time, but then she saw her parents on the front row in the field; they looked up at her with fear and hope.

She had never defended a condemned man before the court. She had the elements she needed to liberate this man, whose face she didn't dare to see; she knew looking at him would jumble the arguments she had prepared with such meticulous care. This was the last and the final chance for this man, who sat still before her, while the stern-faced judges waited to hear what more she had to say over what they already knew about him.

What used to be public before had become personal now.

She recalled her father's words: the pitfalls for the defense attorney in having feelings for the defendant. She looked at her father; she looked at the judges; she looked at the man who had signed the papers over to her for his defense and now sat at the box with no doubts on his face; he had trusted his fate to her hands in full confidence and faith.

She took that as her starting point.

She left her legal arguments aside and spoke to the judges as if they were jurors. The murmurs died around the podium. Between her words, the wind sounded among the corns, the mustards, and the sunflowers in the field. She spoke louder. The wind came sharper. The judges' robes blew away one after another; jurors in civilian clothes emerged.

Except for one woman; she held onto to her judge's robe.

All eyes focused on this woman.

And this woman kept her face lowered.

Lucy stepped closer to the box of jurors; the woman refused to look at her. Lucy reached the box, leaned over its edge, and peered into this woman's eyes. The woman lifted her face and returned Lucy's stare; Lucy saw she was looking at herself in the mirror.

Lucy sprang back in horror.

From the corner of her eyes, she saw her father rising from his seat and then walking toward her on the podium. A gentle hand pressed down on her shoulder from behind. A firm voice spoke soft words in her ear. They told her about the guilt of doubts in justice. They showed her the tears of compassion in the eyes of the code.

Lucy shuddered.

The hand squeezed her shoulder. She lifted her arm, placed her palm over that hand, and felt the texture and the temperature she knew. Her eyes opened. She saw her father leaning over and peering into her.

"They found Arnault," he said.

"Pardon?"

"You heard it."

"Where's he?"

"They didn't say."

"Is he alright?"

"He's alive."

Lucy sat up.

Her father told her she had slept thirteen hours in a stretch. Time had come for her to leave the hospital, go back to her flat, and get ready for Arnault; he would need her help now. Her mother was getting their car from the garage, and he was going over to the doctors for her release. He asked Lucy to pack her stuff then scurried out the door.

20

The channels repeated the story and flashed the images of his recovery, but they didn't say a word more about the injured lawyer; Arnault wondered what had happened to her since they took her to the emergency. One of the gendarmes who guarded his door entered the room. He bowed to Arnault then announced that the colleagues from his rescue squad were coming.

Arnault sat up, thanked this officer, and turned off the television.

The captain of their squad and two of his subordinates showed their cards to the gendarmes, then entered the room and stood at the end of his bed. Arnault reached out and shook their hands. His boss opened the duffle bag slung from his shoulder, took out a new set of uniform, and placed it at Arnault's feet. Then he opened a folder he was carrying, took out a memo bearing the seal of the Republique, and handed it over to Arnault.

Arnault read the note from the president.

His boss informed that the state would charge Arnault for manslaughter, but, with this note from the president and with the testimonies from that woman he had saved, he would never go to a trial or stay suspended from his service.

The law, however, required him to appear before a judge.

Given Arnault's intervention had occurred in the jurisdiction of Paris, a representative from the bureau of public defenders there would be present during his meeting with the judge; a message from the president's office had already gone to that bureau in this regard. His boss took his cell phone out, dialed a number, and passed the phone to Arnault.

A woman answered. Arnault gave his name and told her the purpose of his call. The woman listened in silence, asked him to wait, and then put the call on hold.

Lucy's cell phone rang. She took her phone out and answered the call.

The caller didn't introduce himself. His hoarse voice announced he needed a lawyer to defend him before the judge for a charge of manslaughter. Lucy told him she was on leave for now; he should call her office and get one of his colleagues to represent him.

The caller spoke up.

He excused himself for interrupting her. He stated he had called the office of public defenders in Paris and his call had been transferred to her by mistake. Lucy recognized the deformed voice now. She saw her father nodding at the wheel; she realized where this charge for manslaughter had come from.

"Arnault?"

"Yes?"

"This is Lucy."

"Pardon?"

"I work for that office now."

A long silence followed. Lucy took the phone off her ear then stared at its screen. She had mobile cover, the line still connected her to Arnault, but she didn't hear any sounds from his side. Her father slowed the car, then pulled away to the side of the road and stopped the vehicle on the shoulder.

"Arnault, are you there?"

"Yes."

"Give me your address."

"Of the squad?"

"No," she said. "The hospital."

"Why?"

"To sign your papers."

"Right now?"

"Yes."

Her vision blurred. She scribbled the address then hung up the call.

She strained her eyes at the front seats. Her father squeezed his lips and drummed his fingers on the wheel. Her mother sniffled and blew her nose. Lucy felt the spasm coming up her chest; she rolled down the window and turned her face out.

Her bleared eyes cleared.

The setting sun glittered in the ripples of the Seine and glowed over the bridge that would take her over to Arnault.

Printed in Great Britain
by Amazon